A PASSION THAT COULD NOT BE DENIED...

As Mike undressed before her, Lauren could not take her eyes from his body. She had seen it when they swam in the pool, but this disrobing was a thousand times more erotic. Then he came to stand beside her.

"May I leave the lights on, Lauren?" he asked. And when she would have objected, fearing that her body would disappoint him, he said, "Please, you are so lovely," and she could not deny him as he took her into his arms and drew her down on the bed....

Lauren knew it was too soon to risk the pride and purpose she had so painfully gained—and too late to stop what was happening now....

LISA MOORE raised three children and was a professor of English for twenty years before devoting herself full-time to her career as a writer. She loves traveling and writing, and combines the two to make sure her settings are authentic and colorful.

Dear Reader:

The editors of Rapture Romance have only one thing to say—thank you! Your response to our authors, both the newcomers and the established favorites, has been enthusiastic and loyal, and we, who love our books, appreciate it.

We are committed to bringing you romances after your own heart, with the tender sensuality you've asked for and the quality you deserve. We hope that you will continue to enjoy all six Rapture Romances each month as much as we enjoy bringing them to you.

To tell you about upcoming books, introduce you to the authors, and give you an inside look at the world of Rapture Romance, we have started a free monthly newsletter. Just write to *The Rapture Reader* at the address shown below, and we will be happy to send you each issue.

And please keep writing to us! Your comments and letters have already helped us to bring you better and better books—the kind *you* want—and we depend on them. Of course, our authors also eagerly await your letters. While we can't give out their addresses, we are happy to forward any mail—writers need to hear from their fans!

Happy reading!

Robin Grunder, Editor
Rapture Romance
New American Library
1633 Broadway
New York, NY 10019

SEPTEMBER SONG

by
Lisa Moore

RAPTURE ROMANCE
NEW AMERICAN LIBRARY

PUBLISHER'S NOTE

This novel is a work of fiction. Names, characters, places, and incidents either are the product of the author's imagination or are used fictitiously, and any resemblance to actual persons, living or dead, events, or locales is entirely coincidental.

SIGNET, SIGNET CLASSIC, MENTOR, PLUME, MERIDIAN AND NAL BOOKS
are published by The New American Library, Inc.,
1633 Broadway, New York, New York 10019

First Printing, January, 1984

1 2 3 4 5 6 7 8 9

PRINTED IN THE UNITED STATES OF AMERICA

A salute to
the greatest luxury liner afloat:
the incomparable Queen Elizabeth II

Chapter One

∼

A glistening black limousine drew up in front of the Ocean Passenger Terminal in New York, where the bright star of the Cunard Line, the *Queen Elizabeth II,* was waiting at Berth 4 to begin her five-and-a-half-day cruise to England. A short, stocky man jumped out of the car and gave a hand to his three female companions. These women, all apparently in their mid-thirties, were so striking that even the crowd of hurrying, preoccupied travelers paused a moment to gape at their beautiful, well-dressed figures. As they stood on the sidewalk, there was a seductiveness about them that claimed the eye as surely as their delicate perfume tantalized the nostrils. The stocky man and the chauffeur began to deal with the suitcases.

Lauren Rose beckoned smilingly to two porters. "Over here, please!"

"Damn it, Lauren, you'll never get—" began Herbert Masen crossly. Then he paused, mouth open, as the two porters hurried up to the limo and began piling suitcases onto their trolleys.

Lauren twinkled her demure smile at her late husband's best friend. "You shouldn't underrate the power of two of L.A.'s most glamorous models, Herbert."

Herbert grunted. "To say nothing of yourself, Lauren. That's a damned fetching outfit you've got on," he added, his eyes busy with her lovely figure. Then he spoiled the compliment by adding, "Good idea to have all three of you wearing your designs. It should promote sales."

Lauren herded her two models, who were weary and yawning from the ordeal of a night flight from Los Angeles, into the elevator that led up to the main floor of the terminal's vast, crowded reception area. Herbert began fussing about their tickets and passports.

Lauren said firmly, "Herbert, will you entertain Nella and Dani while I get things organized? Give them some Perrier, or a flower or something. *Not candy or coffee.* I'll pick them up in the waiting room in twenty minutes, Scout's honor."

Herbert gave her his self-conscious little smirk, which usually meant he was up to something. Lauren drew a steadying breath. Her late husband's oldest friend had insisted upon accompanying her to New York, to the very dockside. His concern for her welfare, however, was of such a fidgety, tense nature that she had wished several times since they left Los Angeles that she'd refused his help at the start. An uncomfortable suspicion had crept into her mind as he continued to suggest actions that invariably delayed or hindered her plans. Was Herbert Masen trying to sabotage the most exciting opportunity Lauren had ever had?

She had been invited to present her whole new collection to that little group of American women who set the trend for all the fashion-conscious females in the country. But why would Herbert wish to place obstacles in her way? He had shares in the company her former husband had started to showcase his wife's talents. Since her line—the sophisticated and flattering September Song—had firmly found its market in women in their thirties who were tired of buying dresses designed for eighteen-year-olds, Herbert had shared in the slowly increasing dividends.

Still, there had been pressures. Soon after Al's death, Herbert had urged her to take him into partnership. When she refused, he had been even more insistent that Lauren sell the boutique, the workshop, the name and goodwill she had earned for her line of clothing and accessories—and marry him!

"We'll put your money and mine into a Swiss account," he had proposed one evening after he had wined and dined her lavishly at the Los Angeles Bonaventure Hotel. "Then we'll go and live on the French Riviera." He wiped gravy from his beef Wellington off his lips after he spoke.

Looking at his puffy face, red and shiny with his enthusiasm for his food, Lauren had finally decided that she must break the connection with him entirely. Herbert had been Al's friend, never hers. She didn't even like him. She would gradually stop seeing him.

Easier planned than done. Although she refused all his invitations, Herbert kept dropping in at the house, at the boutique, even at the homes of friends when he learned she would be there. When the New York office of a London publicity firm had asked her to bring her models and her new collection to take part in a glamorous Fashion Cruise on the superb *Queen Elizabeth II*, Lauren had been both excited by the challenge to her skills as a designer and glad for the opportunity to get away from Herbert Masen until he'd found a new interest.

Pulling herself together quickly with the reminder that the Ocean Passenger Terminal in New York was no place to stand and ruminate, Lauren checked with a member of the purser's staff to be sure that her sealed rack of costumes had been delivered aboard and was safely locked in her suite. Then she presented passports and tickets at the appropriate counters. She was instructed to collect her two models for check in, and did so with some trepidation. Nella had been fretting all night long on the plane about what a poor sailor she probably was, and Dani had spent the time flirting with every personable male in sight. Lauren had a grim suspicion that her troubles were only starting.

She was exasperated to find that Herbert had bought queasy Nella and Dani a sandwich and a Coke from the dispensers. "Are you crazy?" she asked the models, holding out her hands for the thick, greasy packages. "If you get mayonnaise on those suits, I'll kill you. Don't you remember there are photographers waiting at the gangway?" She glared at Herbert. "Are you doing this deliberately, Masen?"

"Doing what?" His voice, his narrow smile, were too innocent.

"Good-*bye*, Herbert," Lauren said grimly. "I'll try to forget your help."

She shepherded Nella and Dani through Immigration and led them up to the embarkation hall. A dozen photographers rushed toward them, calling out a babble of instructions to the models. Nella and Dani moved automatically into a series of graceful, elegant, and provocative postures. Dani sparkled at the lenses, her dark curls gleaming, her small figure moving seductively. Nella, tall and big-busted, went into a rehearsed sequence of movements that showed off her statuesque figure as well as Lauren's designs.

Lauren drew in a deep breath of relief. The models were professionals. In spite of their weariness, confusion, lack of sleep and food, and especially in spite of Herbert Masen's efforts, the Lauren Rose September Song mannequins were triumphantly displaying the top numbers of this year's line. And in her own suite on board, safely locked away, were the new designs, the new collection that would, she hoped, win the admiration of fashion-conscious women over thirty years of age. It was thrilling to watch her two models turn and sway and smile, smoky-eyed and beguiling, and to see how gracefully her dresses clung and flowed, glorifying the women's figures. Lauren exhaled a deep breath of satisfaction.

At that minute, a gray-haired reporter approached her. "Who are you?" His question wasn't insolent, merely routine.

"Lauren Rose, September Song Line, Los Angeles." Lauren handed him a small publicity package. She held out her hand with the smile that had won her the friendship and loyalty of her employees as well as her many customers. "I'm also wearing one of this year's top sellers." She gestured at her raw-silk suit, a creamy-gold that exactly matched her softly waving hair. The silk scarf at her throat brought out the deep, almost violet-blue of her eyes. "September Song is created for the lovely woman over thirty who has kept both her wits and her figure."

The man chuckled, his brown eyes gleaming with admiration. "Quotable!"

"May I know your name?" Lauren asked. His answer delighted her. "Reb Crowell!" she exclaimed. "We love your columns in California. It's an honor to have you covering us."

His suddenly wicked grin sparkled. "I'll be glad to cover *you* any time," he teased. "Want to hear my opening paragraphs?" At her smiling nod, he declaimed, in the manner of a TV commentator, "At four-forty-five on a bright Sunday afternoon the *QE II*, darling of the international darlings, pet of the jet set, pulled majestically away from the dock and headed out past the

Statue of Liberty—who was green with envy—on a highly publicized voyage, the Fashion Cruise. Seven of America's finest dress designers are on board, with their latest dazzling collections and their world-famous models. The cream of society from Bel Air to Boston has checked into luxurious staterooms on the greatest liner afloat for her five-and-a-half-day cruise from New York to Southampton. Four glamorous afternoons and three glittering evenings will be devoted to the seven individual showings of the most exciting clothes and accessories American creativity and taste can design—a fabulous fashion preview for America's best-dressed women.

"A panel of judges will be chosen from among the first-class passengers on Sunday evening. These fashion-wise experts will attend all seven shows and then, at the Captain's Dinner the last night before docking, the winner will be announced—"

"Don't say it," interrupted Lauren, laughing, as she held up two sets of crossed fingers. "I'm not superstitious, but—"

"What's the correct good-luck phrase for designers?" queried Crowell, grinning. "Break a leg? No, that's show biz. Tear a dress?"

"Go away before you hex my collection," Lauren begged, looking over toward the photographers. "It's time I rescued my models. I do thank you for your encouragement . . . I think?" she added with a mischievous smile.

Crowell grinned at her. "I'll even mention your name."

Still smiling, Lauren got Nella and Dani away from the photographers and onto the deck. She was just looking around for a steward to direct them to their cabins when Dani ran over to a tall, handsome man in a navy blazer, white slacks, and a white yachting cap.

Putting her hand on his arm coaxingly, she pouted up into his amused face.

"Are you the captain?" she asked.

"No, miss, I'm not. Can I get you a steward?"

"I don't know how to find my cabin," Dani said, fluttering her long eyelashes at him.

Lauren set her teeth. This was all she needed: a model on the make! She came up to them with a smile pinned to her lips. "Dani, if you'll come with me, I promise you we'll find your stateroom. It's right next to mine." Then, when the model seemed reluctant to let go the man's arm, she added more firmly, "Nella wants to lie down and you've got to change before dinner."

With a final languishing smile, Dani turned to follow her employer into the lounge. Lauren's exasperated glance caught the outrageous grin on the big man's face. He saluted mockingly.

Lauren's reaction to his grin surprised her. She felt as though she had been touched by a live wire. Her senses were aware of him, alert to every detail of his strong physique . . .

Hold it. She caught herself up abruptly. You've got a job to do.

She found a courteous steward who led them to their suite. Dani prowled around while Lauren tipped and thanked the man and made sure the sealed clothes rack was safe in her stateroom. Nella had subsided into a comfortable chair, looking pale. Lauren checked out the accommodations the promoters had secured for them: a pleasant, small sitting room from either side of which opened a bedroom. The models' cabin had twin beds and a special triple mirror.

Lauren firmly directed the two into their room. "Get ready for dinner," she advised them. "It won't be formal, since this is the first night, but you'll find the other models will be very much on stage. Wear the dark-red velvet shift, Dani. It's perfect with those pretty black curls of yours. Nella, wear the green silk A-line."

"Green!" Nella groaned. She staggered over to her bed. "I'm not sure I'll be up to it tonight, Ms. Rose," she whimpered. "Oh, I think I'm going to be si-i-ick. . . ."

"You can't be sick yet," Dani argued with her. "We're still tied up at the dock."

"Can't I?" asked Nella. Since she was obviously requesting information rather than issuing a challenge, Lauren was able to reassure her.

"I'll get you some Dramamine and you'll be in good shape. The *Queen Elizabeth II* has wonderful stabilizers that keep her steady even in a storm. There really is nothing to be afraid of—"

The words were barely out of her mouth when there was a heavy, blasting roar. Nella screamed and curled up on the bed in a tight huddle.

"It's only the whistle, dopey," Dani said, hanging up her black-and-white suit and sitting down at the dressing table to change her makeup. As Nella rose hesitantly to begin undressing, Lauren went back across the sitting room into her own bedroom. It was the same size as the other and as charmingly decorated and furnished, but it seemed larger because it held only a single bed. Sighing with pleasure, Lauren removed her small, smart cream hat and suit and put them away carefully in the wardrobe. The blue-violet scarf and her shoes came off next. She walked into the tiny bathroom and scrutinized her face in the generous mirror. Her soft, cream-gilt hair was a little crushed by the hat, but a quick brushing would restore its lustrous waves. One of each, she thought. Dani's a roguish small brunette with a charming tangle of shining black curls. Nella is a statuesque redhead. And I am a middle-sized blonde.

As she stared at her violet-blue eyes with their frame of black lashes, the neat nose, which just escaped being too small, and the wide, soft mouth, she suddenly saw, imposed between her and her image, the mocking smile of the dark man in the blazer.

She had never been so instantly aware of a man before. His half-teasing salute was a challenge that had sparked every nerve in her body to alert response. Even now, she was conscious of every detail of his splendid body: his broad shoulders, the strong, full column of his throat, the thick, shining dark hair, the amazing gray eyes that shone like silver. . . .

Cool off, she advised herself. Smiling wryly, she stepped into the shower, then dressed in the violet sheer wool she had chosen to wear for the first night's dinner. The next half-hour was spent in coaxing her models into their dresses and soothing Nella's fears. One thing she said made Lauren very angry. Apparently, Herbert Masen had given poor Nella dire warnings of the agonies and hazards to be expected upon the high seas. So he *had* been trying to sabotage her showing. A minute's thought told Lauren why. If the show was a disaster, she would be more amenable to his offer of marriage and a sale of the boutique and the September Song name. Or so Herbert probably figured. Well, she'd show Mr. Masen. She praised the models lavishly enough to soothe their deep insecurities, then outlined the evening's events clearly for them.

"First we are to go to the captain's dayroom for cocktails. All the other designers and their models will be there, so we will have to keep very quiet about what *we* are going to show."

Nella and Dani nodded solemnly; they knew more than she did about the rivalries and dirty tricks in the fashion business.

Lauren resumed, "Then we go to our own dining room for dinner. There are four dining rooms on the *QE II,* you know." They hadn't, but they nodded again, eyes bright with interest. "After dinner, we meet with the cruise director, who will tell us all the details we need to know about the different presentations, especially our own. Then he'll take us to the lounge where we'll be putting on our show and let us look at the dressing rooms, runway, and stage. They have some scenery if we wish it, also props."

Dani sighed. "Wouldn't it be super if that gorgeous officer we met on deck was the cruise director? I know he fell for me."

In spite of Lauren's fears, Nella and Dani behaved with perfect propriety during the cocktail hour, both nursing a Perrier as they had been instructed. The cruise director turned out to be a woman, to Dani's disappointment. She seemed competent and friendly, and made clear and careful explanations. It was not too surprising to discover that the other six designers had assistants to deal with their models and with the mechanics of the presentations. One or two of them spoke to Lauren, but the rest either ignored her completely or accepted their introduction to her with a patronizing air.

"Who's *she*?" she heard someone ask Carlos de Sevile, the dark, insolent Spaniard who was chief designer for the expensive, exclusive C. M. Landrill chain of department stores based in Los Angeles. Lauren had been introduced to Carlos on several occasions. She lingered behind the two, waiting to hear what de Sevile would say about her.

"Some cheap little dressmaker," Carlos drawled with a heavy accent, which made Lauren smile because she knew he had been born and educated in Los Angeles.

"No competition to us, I assure you." The two men laughed as they accepted a drink from a passing steward.

Lauren walked away without anger. She knew that Landrill's had tried twice to secure her own designing skill, to put September Song garments and accessories under contract exclusively for their chain of stores. Al had always refused, ranting about conglomerates and big business destroying the small, quality boutiques. Lauren had often wondered what his real reasons were.

She had never really understood Al. Her marriage had been a mistake, although she had tried very hard to make it work. Al had always preferred his nights out with the boys, his trips to Vegas or Mexico or Canada with his special male friends. He seemed to have some deep grudge against the world, and in the last few years his anger and resentment had turned against her also. But she must not waste time thinking of that now, she told herself. She collected Nella and Dani to take them to dinner.

They were seated in a spacious, elegant dining room by attentive, smiling stewards, and the models were well pleased. Lauren, who had done her homework, realized that this was not the most posh of the four restaurants, but it suited her very well to keep a low profile at the moment. The table, centered with fresh roses, seated eight. Lauren found their five table companions delightful. When the dining steward had noted everyone's choices from the impressive menu, she introduced herself and her models.

The older of the two men, Derek Strange, presented his party. They were an English dance troupe, returning home after a five-week tour in the United States. Derek Strange and his wife, Violet, were obviously older than Lauren; Tony Carr, lean and handsome, was about her age; Polly and Dolly Darby, twins, were in their early twenties, Lauren judged. Their manners were charming, but Lauren sensed an underlying depression that even their determined, chins-up cheerfulness could not hide. Halfway through the meal, interrupting a debate on the differences between English and American humor, Nella clutched at Lauren's arm.

"The ship is rolling. I can feel it."

Everyone at table stared at the statuesque redhead, who was very pale. The men glanced at each other, frowned, then shugged.

"I don't feel any motion," Dani argued. "You're imagining it."

Lauren got up. "Let me see you to the cabin, Nella," she said gently. "You've had no sleep for nearly thirty-six hours. I'm sure when you're rested you'll feel better."

"I'll stay with these people," said Dani. "I'm not tired."

Lauren glanced at Violet Strange. "Where will you be, later, Mrs. Strange?" she asked softly, helping Nella to her feet.

"Here or the pub on this deck," the woman answered her with a friendly smile. "We'll look after your mannequin as if she were a doll."

"We've got a business meeting after dinner," explained Lauren. "Dani will need to know the stage, dressing rooms—all sorts of details."

"You'll be back before we've finished dinner," Mrs. Strange assured her. "Not to worry."

Lauren got Nella comfortably settled in bed with a cold cloth on her forehead and then sent for a stewardess and requested some Dramamine. The Englishwoman came back in a remarkably short time with some tablets and a glass of water. "Doctor says give her these and she'll be right as rain tomorrow."

"Thank you very much," Lauren replied with real gratitude.

Nella accepted everything docilely. Then she sobbed, "I just know I'm going to be sick. I shouldn't have come."

Within ten minutes, however, she was sleeping peacefully. Lauren hurried back to the dining room. Dani and the dance troupe were still enjoying their dinner, which was superb and served with style. Lauren sat down at the table with relief. In response to their kind queries, she explained that Nella was a bit of a hypochondriac.

"She's a nitwit," Dani announced coldly. "Just because Mr. Masen told her all those stories about storms at sea, she's sure that we'll all drown or something. *Seasick.* It's as calm as an oyster."

The men chuckled. Dinner proceeded without any further problems, and Lauren enjoyed both the food and the service very much. The company of the dance troupe could, she felt, have been pleasant, had it not been for the unhappiness she sensed in them in spite of their attempts to be cheerful.

Finally she turned to Violet Strange. "Is something wrong? Can I help you in any way?"

Violet gave her a wry look. "Is it that plain, then? We were trying to keep a stiff upper lip."

There was a little pause as the waiter served their desserts. Dani had ordered a fruit-and-cream concoction, but Lauren hadn't the heart to object. There had been enough trauma at the table already. When they were eating again, Violet smiled at Lauren. "We expected to be rejoicing at this point. Our tour of your country was most successful. Then yesterday our promoter disappeared with all the receipts from the trip. All he left us was our return tickets. So we're going home broke."

"I'm terribly sorry," breathed Lauren. "What a rotten trick."

Violet shrugged. "It's happened before to dancers and it will again, I've no doubt. But we were good. We deserved our moment of celebration on the ship."

It was time for Lauren and Dani to go to the Royal Court Lounge for their briefing, yet she really hated to leave Violet and the rest of the troupe. "Perhaps we might meet later, at the pub?" Lauren proposed. A vague idea was drifting around in her head. She wanted to think it through clearly before she made a move. So, with smiles exchanged, the dinner party broke up. Lauren was leading Dani out of the dining room when they ran into a stocky man in full evening dress.

"Herbert! What are you doing here?" Lauren demanded.

"Surprise!" Herbert smirked. "I decided you needed me to get you through this cruise."

"You are the last person I need, you—you traitor," snapped Lauren. "Thanks to you, Nella has gone to bed convinced she's seasick, and we've got a show to put on. Just stay away from her, and from me, or I'll—" She stopped for want of a dire-enough threat.

Herbert laughed. "Well, if she can't do the show, you'll make out just about as well as if she could. You can take her place, can't you? You hadn't a hope in hell of winning against the big guns they've got on the program, anyway. Why don't we all just relax and enjoy the trip?"

Lauren could not remember ever being as angry as she was at that moment. Not only had he ruined Nella's usefulness, but he had come on the trip to gloat over Lauren's failure! Getting her voice under control, she told him, "You'll have to excuse us now, Herbert. We're due at a meeting in the Royal Court Lounge—no guests allowed," she ended sharply as he offered an arm to each of the two women.

Lauren led Dani away quickly. When they reached the spacious room where the fashion shows were to take place, Lauren discovered that none of the other designers was present, just their assistants and models. This did not disturb Lauren; in fact, she was secretly amused at the rather snobbish jostling for prestige it implied.

"I'm in no position to be arrogant," she told a worried Dani. "It's my job to see you get the best dressing room and the best help I can give you. At the moment, that's *me*."

Dani gave her a long, level look. "You really are a doll to work for, Ms. Rose," she said, as though just now convinced of the fact. "I always figured I'd rather work for a man, but you don't pull any tricks and you're here to help me when I need you."

"Thank you, Dani." Lauren suppressed a chuckle. "Now let's get you set."

It was easier than Lauren had dared hope, since the assistants, however top-lofty, had to bow to Lauren's superior status. Carlos de Sevile's deputy sent off a frantic note to his employer after Lauren secured for Dani the dressing table in the best position in the room; apparently the assistant had quite forgotten that he and his models wouldn't be backstage when Lauren's September Song line was being shown. The session was nearly over and the cruise director was assuring everyone of her continued assistance when the flamboyant Spanish designer stormed into the lounge.

"What's going on here?" he barked, his gaze darting at once to Lauren's shining gold head. "What are you pulling, Rose?" There was no trace of the fascinating Spanish accent he usually affected.

"I'm just doing my job, buster," she said cheerfully. "Who wants to know?"

Just for a moment, before he realized she was joking, de Sevile's expression was ludicrous with surprise. Then his full mouth tightened and he said angrily, "I'll report you to the judges—"

"For what? I'm just attending to the logistics of the show with my models. We were all invited to come."

"Carlos de Sevile doesn't have to be here in person. I have assistants to do such jobs," he began with insolent emphasis.

Lauren laughed. "So report me for being faithful to my duty and courteous to our hosts," she suggested. Then she added, "You'll look like a fool, of course, but that's nothing new."

She walked away, her gleaming head high, her violet eyes bright with satisfaction.

An awed Dani spoke softly at her shoulder. "You really told that honcho, Ms. Rose. Aren't you afraid he'll hit back?"

"Let him." Lauren was too elated to be cautious. "Things are tough all over! It really did me good to puncture his hot-air balloon."

Dani shook her head. "I've been in the business a long time, Ms. Rose. Better watch out behind you from now on," she warned gloomily. "You've only got me— and yourself, of course—now that Nella's out of it. You'll have to shorten all Nella's stuff if you want me to wear them, and I'll need you backstage to help if I'm to wear both sets of dresses. It's a mess."

Lauren refused to be downcast. "Let's join our dancing friends in the pub, shall we? They've had a worse knock than we have, and they're still smiling. I like them, don't you?"

Dani refused to commit herself. Her own tastes ran to obviously wealthy men, like the handsome fellow in the blazer. "That hunk of man on deck," she murmured soulfully. "I knew he wasn't an employee of Cunard. His blazer was a Bill Blass and his shoes came from Gucci. In my book, he's a ten, maybe even an eleven."

Lauren grinned and led the way to the cozy Crown and Anchor pub with its very British ambience. She found the troupe gathered around a small table at the rear. Derek got up politely to find two more chairs, but Dani told them she was going down to her stateroom. Derek set Lauren's chair between himself and his "storm and strife."

"He means wife, dear," Violet interpreted. "How did the briefing go?"

Lauren told them about de Seville and got them laughing. Then she insisted upon buying a round.

"Why should you, luv?" Derek asked. "We've still got our pocket money."

The others laughed ruefully, but Lauren insisted. "You see," she explained, two dimples very much in evidence beside her soft, wide mouth, "I've got a proposition to make."

"To me, I hope," teased Tony, the younger man who was the lead dancer and choreographer for the troupe.

"To all of you," Lauren said soberly. "You know that one-half of my team is out. I can't take Nella's place, since our figures and coloring are so different, but mostly because I'm needed backstage to help with costume changes and accessories, as Dani has just reminded me." She looked at each of them in turn: Derek was lean, handsome, silver-haired, fortyish; his wife, Violet, was buxom and tall, her hair dyed a silvery blue; Tony had a hard, young-old face crowned with dark hair and must be, she thought, about thirty-five years old. Then there were the twins, one fair and one dark as Dani, in their late twenties with slender dancer's figures, no hips and no bust. But at this moment they were all alike in the keen interest and hope on every face.

"I'd like to hire you to put on my show for me," Lauren said quietly.

There was a moment of stunned silence as all eyes sought Derek, their manager. He frowned. "All of us? But we're not—uh—mannequins," he began, doubtfully.

"All the better." Lauren launched eagerly yet quietly into her plan. "I've drawn the worst spot on the program, Thursday afternoon, when both the audience and the judges will be bored by the presentations. But for me, Thursday's a good time because it gives us a chance to work out a show that might catch their attention. I got the idea at dinner tonight." She beamed at them. "You're dancers. You move beautifully. You've got stage presence and a kind of witty gallantry about you—"

The men bowed solemnly across the table at her, and the women smiled. Lauren went on. "I thought, when I saw some of the scenery backstage tonight, that I'd set the scene in a modish boutique, with Dani as a lay figure wearing our showiest dress. It's ivory velvet with a pastel sequin bodice and a multipetaled chiffon skirt. The petals move and separate as the model walks. Oh, it's perfectly modest—almost." She chuckled at their expressions, then continued, "I thought I'd have three cleaning ladies come in to do their nightly thing, and fall in love with the dress. They can lift or help her down from the stand, then admire her as she displays the dress. When she's back on her stand, they move her into an alcove and one of them—whichever the dress fits—comes out wearing it."

She caught the flare of interest in the dancers' eyes. "The other two, doing a double take, then come out wearing my creations, and the three dance along the runway to suitable music, admiring one another and themselves. Do you like it so far?"

"We like it," Tony said firmly. "Where do Derek and I come in?"

Lauren gave him a broad grin. "I knew you'd back me up," she crowed. "You're such good sports, and I'm really in a spot."

"Knights-errant, that's Tony and me," Derek hammed it up. "So what do *we* do?"

"You are night watchmen who come to check out the activity in the dress salon," Lauren told them. "You dance the ladies once down the runway and back to the stage, using steps you, Tony, have choreographed to display my dresses to their best advantage, with appropriate music. Then you men lead the women offstage and lift Dani back to her stand. She'll be wearing my most seductive lingerie. Derek will hastily bring out my high-style evening cape and whirl it around to cover her."

"A little humorous mime there," Derek decided, grinning.

"I love it," Violet gasped.

All the others were equally enthusiastic. "We can handle both the dancing and the mime," Tony said without false modesty. "We'll need to see the costumes, get an idea of the kind of music and dance steps that would show them off to best advantage . . ." he paused, pondering.

Lauren could have hugged them all. "If you're free to come to my suite right now, I'll show you the dresses. I haven't anything for you men to wear, though."

"Chauvinist," Tony gibed.

Derek smiled. "No problem, we've our own costumes. I'll work something out," he said thoughtfully.

They followed Lauren to her suite, where she glanced

into the models' bedroom. Nella was asleep. Dani, as she might have expected, was not present. Lauren led the troupe to her own bedroom and locked the door.

"Just a precaution," she told them. "It's really important that no one—not even my own employees—get any idea of what we're doing. I can't be sure they wouldn't mention it to the wrong people, and we'd have de Sevile screaming to the cruise director or someone."

"We understand all about professional caution and jealousy," Polly said quietly.

After removing the padlock, Lauren zipped open the rack cover from her new collection. Each costume was kept immaculate in its own cover. Quickly Lauren stripped these off and began matching sizes to her new models. To her relief, Violet was just a little heavier than Nella, and about the same height.

"We'll take you to the hairdressing salon and have your hair colored light auburn, if you don't mind too much?" Lauren asked.

"Of course she doesn't." Derek grinned. "It's about time she roused my interest with a new color."

His wife swatted at him. "Enough of your sauce. You could use a new look, too."

"No, I love that silver—so good with formal black," Lauren said. "Do you men have black tights? Then, with security guard patches, that should do for your first entrance. Evening dress for your subsequent appearances, I think."

"They've got tails *and* dinner jackets," Dolly volunteered.

A few minutes later Lauren sat back on her heels from pinning up a hem and sighed her satisfaction. "I must be the luckiest dress designer in the whole U.S.A.," she breathed, beaming up at them. "Dani's things will fit the twins perfectly, with the hems shortened just a tad, and the seams taken in. I thought *models* were slender. Dancers must really diet."

Through indulgent laughter, Polly worried, "That means you'll have to take in all the—uh—"

"Corsages is the polite word, I think," Derek suggested.

"Bodices," Tony corrected him primly.

This was received with laughter by the women, then Lauren said, "Dressmaking is my business, after all, and alterations are a big part of it. September Song clothes aren't styled for immature figures. Actually, you twins are younger than Dani, and less—ah—mature. . . ."

This time it was the men who chuckled. Derek said, with mock complaint, "I really cannot permit that canard about my wife's figure, Mrs. Rose. Our English word for her is buxom."

"Especially in the corsage," Tony added.

Violet mimed aggression at them both. Lauren found she was feeling very close to them all. They were gallant in disaster. She thanked them again for their help, explained carefully about the age group for which she designed, and apologized to the twins. "You're supposed to be between thirty and thirty-five. Can you mime it?"

"We can act the part—and enjoy it in those clothes," Polly promised eagerly. "They're an inspiration to be thirty."

"To wear those dresses," Dolly agreed, "I'd pretend to be seventy."

The troupe expressed satisfaction with the salary Lauren was able to offer them. They were eager to get started, and began to point out various dresses and suggest music and choreography. In fact, Tony had already found an old envelope in his pocket and was making notes.

Derek ushered the dancers into the corridor. "We'll be up half the night," he said mock lugubriously. "When Tony gets started setting a dance . . ."

"We'll be in touch tomorrow," Violet promised, "to show you our ideas. Thank you." She pressed Lauren's hand and went after her friends.

Closing the door gently, Lauren leaned against it, trembling with the after effects of tension. She had committed herself and her livelihood to a group of unknown talents. Charming and professional as they all seemed, how could she know whether their dancing and mime would enhance her costumes or make them look ridiculous? The trembling became a violent shaking. Lauren gasped for breath. Suddenly the cabin seemed to close in on her, to be airless. Catching up her coat, Lauren left the room, locking the door behind her, and made her way up to the deck.

It was dark and windy, and at first she thought she was alone. She walked quickly to the rail and grasped its comforting hardness with shaking hands. She forced herself to breathe deeply, desperately seeking to absorb the tranquillity promised by the vast, quiet ocean and the clear moonlight.

And then she became aware of a human presence behind her, felt it with a sharp alertness, an immediate sensory perception that struck into her consciousness like a dazzling light. The first assault was to her sense of smell. A tantalizing mixture of spice and the musky redolence of a man's clean, warm body drifted to her nostrils. Next there was the moisture of breath against her neck, and the heat radiating from a large body close to her back. Her own skin, in spite of her coat, was cold in the night air; the contrast between her chill and this new warmth was disturbing. Lauren stood very still. She had never been so sharply aware of another person in her life. She turned slowly to face whoever was standing behind her.

She found herself face to face with the man whom Dani had accosted as they were boarding, the man whose mocking smile had taken note of her exasperation at the model's behavior. Instead of the blazer, he was now wearing a beautiful, form-fitting dinner jacket with a soft white shirt and black tie. He was taller than she remembered, and loomed over her with his powerful chest and shoulders, his dark head bent toward her as he stared at her. The moonlight turned his eyes to liquid silver.

And then his voice sounded in her ears, deep and dark like the ocean depths, but warmer, *warmer* . . . a husky voice, as erotic as the rasp of black velvet against the fingertips.

"Are you all right, Mrs. Rose? Can I help you?"

Lauren caught her breath, then held her voice steady as she answered, "Thank you, no, I'm fine. I was . . . feeling a little tired, but it's not surprising, really. I haven't slept in over thirty-six hours." She tried for an easy, casual laugh. "Jet lag?"

"Not enough proper food to eat and too much responsibility, wouldn't you say?" he answered, astonishing her.

That touch of condescending male chauvinism was just the stimulation Lauren so desperately needed. Her head lifted and she stared up into the dark face above her. "I've been carrying a fairly heavy load of responsibility for a number of years now, Mr.—?" she waited with an intense curiosity she didn't understand to hear him name himself.

But he threw her off balance again when, instead of

giving her his name, he said abruptly, "With, of course, the help of Mr. Herbert Masen."

"Herbert?" Lauren's voice broke into scornful laughter. "All Herbert does is complicate the issue. He's determined I'll—" She broke off, unwilling to share any more of her private concerns with this man, even if he did seem to know a surprising amount about her affairs. Better to confront him at once, she decided. "Just who are you? And how do you happen to know so much about me?"

"I've been listening to your Mr. Masen in the bar for the last hour. He told me he is willing to marry you in spite of the mess you are making of your fashion presentation. Then you will sell your boutique and the rights to your designer clothes, after which you both plan to laze away the rest of your lives following the jet set from one resort to another. With *you* footing the bills."

Lauren's scorn was evident in her voice. "You think I've agreed to that repulsive little scenario?"

"Well," the man drawled insolently, "One would hope not, of course. But I have noticed that you can't control your models."

Lauren set her jaw against an angry retort. In a moment, she said quietly, "I've controlled my employees and marketed my designs successfully for ten years. Perhaps both you and your drinking buddy have something to learn about me. Now if you'll excuse me—" She tried to move past him toward the interior of the ship.

Instantly he was in front of her again. He didn't touch her, but she felt the force of him on her senses as she had before, and something more—a sort of recognition, a familiarity. He was speaking again, but this time the deep, caressing voice held neither insolence nor condescension.

"You don't think this is a chance meeting, do you? I've been looking for you all night on a matter of business."

Lauren stared up at the unsmiling face. Moonlight emphasized the sharp planes of his face and sparkled in his silver eyes. He went on speaking.

"It seems I may have been wrong. You don't fit the picture Masen drew of you. But you *are* having trouble with the details of your presentation, are you not? You've got the worst time slot on the program. One of your models is sick and the other man-crazy, and Masen says Carlos calls your designs trashy."

Lauren drew a deep breath. "Perhaps you and Masen should wait until the votes are counted before you trash me," she said. "Or you might try to find a more reliable spy. I'm putting on a show, Mr. Anonymous, and neither Masen nor Carlos de Sevile is going to stop me."

Suddenly, he caught her by the wrist. "Forgive me. I can see that the half was not told me. I admit there's no excuse for my behavior. It was just that I got angry at what I thought you were doing with your chance to show your designs. May we start again, please, with a clean slate? Maybe I can help you."

But Lauren had had enough. "I can handle it, thank you." The confidence she had in Derek's troupe and her own skills sounded in her voice. "Carlos and Masen are in for a surprise."

"I'd really like to help," he repeated. "My name's Michael. May I just stand by you here for a few minutes to enjoy the night air? Will you have a cigarette?"

Lauren found herself relaxing at his evident eagerness to make amends. "Thank you, no, I don't smoke. But I would like to stay on deck for just a little longer. It's relaxing; the sea is so big and dark and *ancient* . . .

He moved to the rail beside her. Sharing a comfortable silence, they leaned on the rail, their bodies just touching, and looked outward across the moving darkness. Then, as they kept vigil, a lovely sight met their eyes. At a good distance to the south they saw a glow of light that, as they watched, became a toy ship plowing past them, westward to New York, sparkling and beautiful against the dark of night and sea. They watched it until its lights were once more a misty blur. Then a cold wind swept against Lauren and she shivered.

Michael put a hard, warm hand over hers on the rail.

"All those people on the other ship," Lauren whispered. "Don't you feel as though you could almost *touch* them? How I wish I knew them all—their life stories, their fears and dreams, what each one is hoping for as they race toward New York."

He caught her against his side with a strong, friendly arm.

"What a romantic you are. And here I thought Lauren Rose was a hard-hearted, grasping businesswoman." He was teasing her, but his voice was still gentle. "You'd better deal with your problems on this ship before you try to comprehend those of the rest of the world." He gave her a brief, hard hug that Lauren found oddly comforting from a stranger. "Now, to bed! Or the designer of the September Song line will never be alert enough to organize her fashion showing." He led her back inside. "May I get you some wine? Cocoa?" he wheedled, grinning.

Lauren knew it was definitely time she removed herself from the clutches of this wily charmer. Slipping out from under his arm, she smiled up into his laughing countenance. "Good night," she said firmly. *"Good night."*

He caught her hand.

" 'Parting is such sweet sorrow,' " he teased, his gray

eyes luminous with laughter. "Now *my* line is 'Sleep dwell upon thine eyes . . .' And then how does it go?"

A Shakespeare buff as well as everything else, Lauren groaned silently. This guy was too much. Could he be an actor? He was good-looking enough, and he certainly had *presence*.

He was speaking again, declaiming, his arresting voice full of amusement, and something else. " 'Peace in thy breast! Would I were sleep and peace, so sweet to rest!' "

His eyes went boldly to the violet wool draped so snugly over Lauren's rounded breasts as he quoted those provocative words of Romeo's. He moved toward her quickly, but Lauren slipped from his grip and walked down the corridor toward her stateroom.

As she went, she told herself that this man could be very dangerous to her peace of mind. He was wildly attractive, and he certainly knew it. The knowledge was in the wicked glint in his gray eyes, in the wide, challenging smile that made a woman so much aware of his masculinity—and her own feminine response to it. Women probably spoil him rotten, she mused, turning into her own entry hallway. Better be careful he doesn't get under my guard.

She hadn't had time to be lonely since Al's death, and she hadn't been accustomed to much male attention for the last few years of their marriage. Al had been busy making the boutique go, and he liked to spend his free time with his men friends—"getting away from the hassle," he called it.

You're ripe for somebody like Michael, she warned herself. Don't be a pushover. You don't know this guy from Adam. He might even be a pal of de Sevile's.

She opened the door to the sitting room and halted on the threshold, surprise and anger battling for supremacy. Herbert was sprawled on the couch, glaring foolishly at her. His red face and slightly glazed eyes told the story. Before she could speak, he said, with slurred speech, "Where've you been? Who with?"

It had been a long forty hours. And the pressure breaking down Lauren's patience with Herbert's sly, malicious tricks had been building up even longer. Her voice shook with rage. "It's none of your damned business, Masen. Now get out of here and don't come back."

Herbert staggered to his feet, scowling. "I don't have to put up with—"

Lauren was ready to hit him. "Get out!" She held the door open and stood aside.

With a ludicrous attempt at dignity, Herbert stalked past her.

Lauren locked the door after him. Tomorrow she'd warn Nella and Dani never to leave that door, or their own door to the corridor, unlocked. Herbert's expression had been vindictive. The new collection was in her room. Each of them had a key; it had to be that way. She wasn't their mother or their keeper. But the doors must be kept locked to protect the dresses. Lauren was so worried that she opened the models' door quietly, to warn Dani if she were still awake.

Nella slumbered peacefully. Dani's bed had not been touched. With a sigh that was half a groan, Lauren went to her own bedroom. It was only as she was drifting off to sleep that she recalled something Michael had said. It had not been a chance meeting. He had been looking for her "on a matter of business." De Sevile's business?

Chapter Two

Lauren woke early Monday morning. The cabin sparkling with sunlight, the salty breeze from the open porthole, the fresh smell of varnish, clean linen and the lavender soaps in the bathroom, it all roused Lauren so completely she was practically forced out of bed. She looked at her small traveling alarm and saw it was six A.M. Then, she recalled the pool on deck and things didn't seem so bad; the idea of a wake-up swim quite appealed to her. Surely few others would be using it so early on the first morning of the trip? Smiling at her own adolescent impulse, Lauren got into her swim suit and robe, slipped on some deck shoes, picked up a towel, and went in search of the pool.

A big man was doing laps as she approached. All Lauren could see was a dark, wet head, bronzed arms flashing in a strong Australian crawl, and the froth of water from powerful leg beats. She dropped her robe and towel on a deck chair, slipped off her shoes, and dived in neatly. When she came to the surface, she was almost face to face with the other swimmer. With a sense that she was fate's helpless pawn, she recognized him.

Michael, treading water near her, grinned at her surprise.

"Looks as though we have similar tastes, or the same health guru," he said.

"How many laps have you done?" Lauren asked, struggling for composure. Michael, seen like this, was a devastatingly handsome figure of strength and physical beauty, and she suddenly felt acutely self-conscious being so close to him.

"Ten," he said. "Want me to wait till you catch up?"

"That's a good handicap," Lauren said rashly. "I'll race you one lap."

His raised eyebrows hardened her resolve. Then he smiled, a slow, warm smile that made her want to touch his wet cheek with her hand. "You're on. We'll start from a racing dive at that end."

He swung up easily onto the deck, then pulled her smoothly up beside him. "You call it," he offered.

Lauren took her stance. "One two, three—dive!"

She sensed that he hit the water a fraction of a second later than she did. He had given her that small advantage, but he wouldn't hold back, she thought. Then all conscious thought was suspended as Lauren worked her body through the water with every ounce of skill and training and willpower she had. She might not win, but by God, Michael would know he had been in a race.

She reached the end of the pool too quickly and twisted into her best racing turn. As she flashed out for the return length, she caught a glimpse of a bronze arm cutting the air a few feet away. Michael was level with her. Grimly Lauren stroked, giving it the extra surge her swim coach had taught her to use. Michael didn't know it, but he was racing with a girl who might have made the Olympic team at sixteen, if her parents had not refused to permit her to attempt to qualify.

And she'd spent an hour swimming nearly every day of her adult life.

She slapped her hand on the edge of the pool, only to see a big brown hand come down at exactly the same minute. Then, panting and starting to laugh helplessly, they clung to the deck and faced each other.

"You are some classy lady, Lauren Rose," Michael said, pushing his black hair off his forehead. "And before you ask me, no, I didn't let you win."

"You could have beaten me if the pool were a couple of meters longer," Lauren admitted. "That was my best effort."

Michael shook his head admiringly. "It was good. I had no idea I was in the company of a swimming master, or is it mistress?" he amended, with the warm, wide grin. "Want to go another few laps for fun?"

Lauren was suddenly tired. "I'll give it a pass this time," she said, turning to the ladder.

Michael swung up on the deck and extended both hands. "Want a lift?"

She didn't, actually. The sight of that wet, bronzed body, firm and well-muscled, with a mat of black hair tapering down to his brief black trunks like an arrow sent alarms off along her nerves. She really didn't know who he was, or what had been his purpose in looking for her the night before. Still, she had to admit he hadn't sought her out this morning. She'd found him. Taking his hands, she drove down powerfully with her feet as he lifted. She shot up onto the deck in a movement as graceful as a ballet dancer's.

He caught and held her for just a moment, to make sure she was steady on her feet. That brief contact of wet skin to bare wet skin sent a charge through Lauren's body. It had been a long time, she realized, since she had felt just that special thrill of awareness of a male.

No, to be honest, she had never felt it before. Whatever Al's other strengths, he had never made her so conscious of her sexuality—so aware of herself and almost frightened. She turned quickly to pick up her towel.

"You're very beautiful." The deep voice was softly abrasive, stirring her to unwilling response. She peered at him above the towel she was drying her face with. He wasn't smiling; his gray eyes were openly assessing as much of her body as he could see. Lauren remembered she was wearing one of her own designs, a one-piece, well-cut-out suit that flattered a full figure more than a bikini did. It was a curving blend of violet, blue, and rose in a flowing line that made the most of her rounded breasts and hips without neglecting her small waist. It was short enough to make her legs look long and graceful. It gave her confidence now, in the face of the man's declaration of her beauty.

"Thank you," she said simply, with a rather tentative smile.

"I wish you'd call me Mike," he requested.

"Thanks for a good workout, Mike," Lauren said, catching up her robe and thrusting her arms into it.

"Don't forget your shoes," he reminded her, bending to pick them up. "Sit down."

Almost unthinkingly, Lauren obeyed him. He knelt and, taking her towel from her hand, began to dry her feet carefully.

Lauren drew in her breath. It was the most erotic experience—the feel of those large, strong hands holding her feet and rubbing them firmly with the towel. When he dried each toe separately in a gentle, sensual caress, hot color came into Lauren's cheeks. Of course he chose that moment to look up at her, his gray eyes intent.

If he laughs at me, I'll sock him, Lauren promised herself.

Even more disturbingly, Mike didn't laugh. His glance touched her face, her breasts, and then returned to her feet. Satisfied that he had them dry, he put the deck shoes on carefully, patting each foot as he had it shod. Then he leaned back on his heels and grinned at her.

"That's a good girl," he approved. "Now you can get dressed."

Lauren left him without another word.

Before she faced anyone, especially the sharp-eyed Dani, Lauren knew she would have to get herself together. As she showered and dressed, she told herself sternly that she was no callow ingenue, fluttering over a handsome male body and a challenging smile. She was thirty-five, damn it. A strong, healthy, beautiful thirty-five, a good businesswoman and a top-notch designer. Why was she dithering like some sixteen-year-old? Glancing critically at herself in the mirror over her dressing table, she saw a woman in a simple-looking, cream silk dress that moved lovingly over every rounded curve. The armholes were bound with violet silk, the belt and scarf were two more of her signature violet silk scarves. Her eyes—stormy dark, almost purple—flashed in her sweet peach-golden face. Lauren squared her shoulders. "Here I come, world," she muttered. "I'm going to put on the best show ever."

She went on deck to walk off her tension before she ate breakfast. As she was returning to the lounge, she noticed a young woman wearing high heels, instead of the more suitable deck shoes. Just as they met, the girl's heel caught on the raised sill of the door leading out to the deck. Lauren thrust out her arms instinctively and caught her before she fell.

"Oh, thank you," gasped the girl as Lauren helped her regain her balance.

"Are you all right? You'll find rubber-soled shoes are much more comfortable, and safer, than heels." Lauren smiled and would have passed on, but the girl caught her arm.

"You're one of the models, aren't you?" she asked. "I saw you last night at the Captain's party. I'm Gala Devine. I work for Carlos de Sevile."

"How do you do, Gala," Lauren said, meeting her smile warmly. "I'm Lauren Rose, with the September Song line."

Gala—the name seemed appropriate for a de Sevile model, Lauren thought cattily—tried out her ankle and then clung to Lauren's arm. "Gee, I hope I haven't strained it. Señor Carlos will kill me."

"Does it hurt? Perhaps we should get you to the doctor," Lauren suggested.

Gala tried a few steps, holding on to the other woman's arm. "No, I think it's just a little sore. Have you had breakfast?"

"I'm on my way there. We eat at Tables of the World restaurant—"

"So do we," Gala said with a smile. "Not Señor de Sevile, of course, but his models, all but the top two. They go to dinner with him at the new Princess Grill Restaurant."

Lauren allowed herself to look suitably impressed, and suggested that they go down to their own restaurant together. Gala was a cheerful child, but something seemed to be worrying her. Over the spartan breakfast she allowed herself, she broached the problem to Lauren.

"What's wrong with my dress, Lauren?" she asked.

"Is it a de Sevile?" countered Lauren cautiously. She didn't like it and knew why, but it might not be diplomatic to make a disparaging comment that might get back to the designer.

"Yes, it's one of his Sevillana Line. They're all like this—heavy reds and purples and black and this trim." Gala held up her slashed red-and-purple sleeve, showing Lauren the tiny white bobbles of cotton that trimmed its fringe.

Lauren decided to level with Gala.

"You know I'm one of de Sevile's competitors, Gala. He doesn't worry about me, but I wouldn't like him to think I'm criticising his designs."

Gala nodded, frowning. "But it's just between us models, isn't it? I wouldn't pass it along. Please, what's wrong with it?"

Lauren gave in. The girl had taste, or awareness of what looked good on her thin, lithe frame. And it wasn't that dress!

"Well, Gala, you're quite slender. That style is too mature for you, too heavy-looking."

"All the Sevillana Line is like this," Gala muttered discontentedly. "Señor de Sevile—he insists we all call him that, not Mr.—doesn't seem to care what age women are, he just designs what *he* likes. This season's clothes were all red, black, orange, and purple. They're loose on the breasts on most of us. Models are thin, Lauren. Everyone knows that. But his clothes are cut full on top, tight to below the hips, and then they flare out with lots of ruffles. I don't like them. They only look good on Dolores, his top model."

Lauren had to agree. She said cautiously, "The colors are hard to wear, but you're young enough to get away with them. It's a Spanish-inspired line, isn't it? Perhaps that's why he makes the clothes that we associate with flamenco dancers, tight to the hips and ruffled below."

Gala sighed. "I like what you're wearing." She shifted

in her seat and suddenly winced. "I think I *will* go look up the doc. Señor de Sevile will kill me if I turn up limping tomorrow evening for his showing."

"*Olé,*" murmured Lauren as the girl walked gingerly away from the table.

She was just finishing her coffee when the dance troupe came into the dining room. They were all beaming, a delightfully different mood than the one they had been in the night before.

"We've got a room with a piano to practice in," Violet announced. "And the door locks," added Derek.

"Will you need any of us for fittings?" asked Dolly.

Lauren set a time, thanked them with a wide smile for their assistance, and turned to go. As she passed a nearby table, a man stood up, as though he had been waiting for her. Mike took her arm and led her out of the restaurant.

"I hope you'll forgive me." He grinned. "I overheard your comments just now, and you're right. That pretty little model really doesn't suit that flamboyant costume. She looks as though she's wearing mommy's dress."

If he were one of de Sevile's spies, Mike would talk exactly like that, Lauren knew. On the other hand, he might be a roving reporter out for a juicy designers' war story. She looked at him doubtfully. "How do you fit into this, Mike? What's your line?"

"I'm an entrepreneur, talent scout, manager—you name it." He laughed softly. "What's your verdict on that dress, Lauren?"

"It's a Sevillana, Gala tells me," Lauren stalled. "I think it's probably featured in Landrill's High Kick boutiques for young women."

"What do you think of it?" Mike persisted.

Lauren shrugged. "Carlos's designs don't try to en-hance the wearer; they shout Carlos. I recognized the color combinations and line of the costume before Gala told me," Lauren admitted. "His dresses are quite good on some eighteen-year-olds—dark, Spanish types with very full figures—but they're disastrous for slender, blonde teenagers and for most American women over thirty. They also cost so much that only wealthy women can afford them." She glanced at Mike with a smile. "I hope you're taking this with a pound of salt, Mike. I'm Carlos's rival, if only in a very humble way. It could be professional jealousy talking."

Mike shook his head, his eyes intent on her laughing countenance. "Somehow I don't think so," he mused. "You certainly know what suits *you*, and your models present a most attractive image. Why don't you tie up with one of the big companies, Lauren? Saks or Bullocks or Landrill's? Free yourself to create, and let someone else run the business end of it?"

"My husband did have offers," Lauren explained. "He seemed very much opposed to handing over our line and my designs to what he called the big conglomerates."

"And what did *you* think? Or didn't Mr. Rose permit you to have any ideas of your own—away from the design board, I mean?"

Lauren frowned. It hadn't been that way, had it? She had always been content to let Al run the business. But she remembered times when she had had to go for a swim in their pool to work off some of the frustrations his autocratic attitudes had roused in her. She shook her head. What did it matter now? She was alone and running the business well—at least the profits were slowly increasing—and loving every minute of it. She put a smile on her face.

"The widow is running her own show, Mike. After this cruise, I may get some offers to sell exclusively to one of the biggees. I'll wait until that time to make a decision."

"Very shrewd, Mrs. Rose." Mike grinned. "So you've got something up your sleeve, have you? Not entirely dependent upon the seasick model or the unreliable one?"

So he'd seen her talking to Derek.

"Dani's not unreliable," Lauren pointed out, defending the girl although she was still worried about her long, late-night absences. Too much of that could ruin both complexion and poise.

"Want some help?" Mike offered lazily. "There really are wolves out there, you know. Things happen."

Lauren held up two sets of crossed fingers. "Bite your tongue," she warned. "I won't let you frighten me."

"Have dinner with me tonight?" he suggested.

"I'm booked." She grinned. "See you later."

She noted the rather regretful look on his handsome face—an endearing little crease at the corners of his finely chiseled mouth—but it only served to send her away more quickly. She mustn't get tied up with a man right now; too much depended upon her keeping her wits about her. And he could be hooked up to any one of the other designers. Maartens wouldn't stoop to unprofessional practices, nor would Adah Shere, she thought, running quickly down the roster of designers as she went toward her suite. Carlos de Sevile certainly would take any advantage he could get, legal or illegal. Of the other three, Telford was too comfortably assured of the preppie trade to bother, Ben Nowak of Chicago was too arrogant and well-established in the mass markets to need an edge, and Janus of San Francisco was only concerned with the cult group it held with its incredibly fine and sensuous leathers.

Lauren shrugged and unlocked the door of the sitting room.

"Who's there?" came Nella's wavering voice from her bedroom.

"Lauren. I've come to see if you'd like a walk on deck before breakfast," Lauren sang out cheerfully.

A groan was the only answer.

Then Dani appeared in the bedroom doorway, heavy-eyed and sloppy in an old woolen dressing gown two sizes too large for her. Lauren smothered a chuckle at the thought of the reaction she'd get if she let Dani model that way.

"Did you sleep well?" she asked blandly.

Dani shot her a suspicious glare. "You know I was out late, Ms. Rose. I met this man in the casino. He was really doing well, raking it in. He said I was bringing him luck, and asked me to stand beside him. After a while he got tired and bought me a few—" She halted, appalled at what she'd nearly said.

"So he bought you a few drinks," Lauren concluded. "Lucky we aren't putting on our show this afternoon."

"Gee, Ms. Rose. Are we going to be able to put a show on at all? Nella claims she's still sick—"

"I've made some other plans," Lauren said firmly. "Oh, you get to model all the dresses that look so good on you, don't worry. But I've found some substitutes for Nella." She returned the girl's incredulous stare with a smile. "It's going to be good, but I've got to keep it under wraps until I'm sure the—the substitutes can handle it." She smiled at Dani's outfit. "You going to wear that number to breakfast? That'll really put de Sevile's mind at rest."

Dani grinned and turned back into the room. "Won't be a minute," she called out, banging the bathroom door.

A groan from Nella acknowledged that insensitivity. Lauren went in to stand beside the woman's bed. She looked gaunt, in spite of her generous curves. She did look ill, and Lauren decided to ask the doctor to call if Nella wasn't back on her feet by dinnertime.

"What can I order for you?" she asked softly. "Some orange juice? Perrier? Tell me, and I'll get it for you."

Nella raised heavy lids. "I'm terribly sorry, Ms. Rose. I know I should have told you before, but I really am afraid of ships and planes." Her voice broke.

Lauren patted her shoulder and smoothed the red hair from her clammy forehead. "I'm going to wash your face and then ask the ship's doctor just to glance at you. There may be something very simple he can do to make you feel a lot better."

Expecting an argument, Lauren was surprised when Nella agreed almost enthusiastically. "Thanks, Ms. Rose. I'll be glad to see the doctor. Should I change out of this gown?"

Feeling a great deal less worried about the model after that speech, Lauren went to the telephone in her bedroom and requested a visit from the ship's doctor at his convenience. Then she returned and helped Nella to wash and don a fresh nightgown. Dani, ready for her breakfast by this time, announced that she'd go ahead, and return to the suite for a briefing after she'd eaten.

"Take a walk around the decks first," Lauren advised. "It's a marvelous day and you probably need the exercise."

When the doctor had come and gone, Lauren went in to see how Nella was doing. She found the model ecstatic.

"Wasn't he wonderful?" Nella breathed. The handsome, middle-aged British doctor had completely won her over. "He says he'll come back this evening to check on my progress."

Lauren groaned. Nella was obviously going to enjoy being sick as long as she could count on visits from the Englishman. "The fashion show," she reminded Nella. "Did he say you'd be able to model the clothes?"

"I forgot to ask," Nella confessed, dreamy-eyed. "Did you notice the way his hair curled around his ears? Yummy!"

Lauren shrugged. Thank God for Derek's troupe. Leaving Nella to her daydreams, she went out to find the practice room the dancers had secured. When she knocked, there was a silence; then the door opened slightly and Tony peered out through the crack. When he saw Lauren, he swung the door wide, pulled her in, and locked the door again.

"Security," he whispered, grinning widely.

"He likes to play Secret Agent X," Polly scoffed.

"He's got the right idea," Lauren advised them. "I know at least one designer who would be delighted at the chance to sabotage my show."

This pronouncement sobered even the twins. Derek said quietly, "Come and see what Tony's done so far. I think you'll like it."

With Violet playing softly at the piano they had managed to borrow from the cruise director, the cast ran through the dances and mime that Tony had already set. Lauren was surprised and delighted. They were very professional, very graceful in movement, and witty with their mime. What had been originally planned as a conventional showing of costumes was now a charming and funny musical comedy. When Lauren tried to express her gratitude, the dancers beamed at her and promised that the finished product would be even better.

"How long have we got?" asked Tony.

"Three days. My showing is scheduled for Thursday afternoon. Does that give you enough time?"

"It's a breeze, luv," Derek said.

"And the music?" Lauren asked. "Have you chosen songs to match the costumes?"

"Waltzes and fox-trots," said Tony, "with just a few classical themes—"

"But please, no tangos." Lauren laughed. "And you won't breathe a word of this, please?"

"Not even to each other," Derek promised. "We'll communicate in mime."

Laughing, they let Lauren out and locked the door after her.

It was nearly lunchtime. Where did the minutes go? Thursday afternoon would be upon her before she knew it. And Mike *had* overheard her when she conferred with the troupe at breakfast. What was his angle? Lauren frowned. Even if he told Carlos and Carlos squawked to the cruise director, what could anyone do? There were no rules about *how* the costumes should be presented. Lauren Rose of September Song had always been known as an innovator, one to break away from stereotypes toward a more body-related, comfortable style. She didn't force her clients into bloomers or Cossack hats just because somebody like Carlos de Sevile decided he liked them on his currently favorite model.

By this time Lauren had reached her suite, and, after a peek at sleeping Nella, she went to her own room, determined to create for herself as glamorous an appearance as possible.

Fifteen minutes later, wearing a violet jump suit that made the most of her petite yet curving figure, she went up to Tables of the World. She had left her creamy-gold hair to wave softly to her shoulders, and knew she looked her best. After a light meal, she went up to the first of the fashion shows in the Royal Court Lounge.

The spacious, elegant room was crowded with smartly dressed women and a number of men. A babble of conversation and laughter greeted Lauren's ears as she glanced around to see if any of the other designers had made themselves visible at the Janus presentation. Carlos was there, she noted, prominently positioned in the first row with a brightly plumaged model on either side of him.

"Prepare for leather," muttered a deep voice at her shoulder.

She didn't need to turn around to recognize Mike. His hand on her elbow seemed to warm her whole body as he guided her to a couch at the back of the lounge. It was set between two very healthy plants, whose generous greenery made a kind of nook out of the space. Lauren sank down thankfully. She hadn't come to be stared at, but to evaluate the total presentation: costumes, movement, music, and any quirks of production that might be innovative.

"What are *you* doing here?" she prodded Mike as he lounged so unselfconsciously beside her. Lauren knew this designer's clothes were nothing like Mike's style. Janus was actually two men; Sidney, who managed the business side of the firm as Al had done, and Jan, the wildly trendy designer. Janus's supple and erotic leathers were the favorite with a whole section of San Francisco's society, a group that had nothing in common with Mike. He was too fully, and traditionally, male. He was so much man that he didn't need to prove it. The immaculate, well-tailored suit he wore so casually emphasized his superbly muscled body. He moved in his clothing, Lauren thought with a designer's awareness, with an efficient grace that was totally masculine.

Given all this, she wondered why he was present at the show. She would have pictured him playing squash or swimming or skeet-shooting, rather than watching fashion presentations. She looked up at his face, her eyes wary. He was watching her, a smile tugging at the corners of his well-cut mouth.

"Maybe I just dropped in on the chance of meeting you," he murmured, reading her mind with an ease that disturbed her.

The models, both male and female, began their stylized strutting on the wide runway that thrust out into the auditorium. The Janus models wore heavy makeup, a sort of unisex mask that went very well with their sensuous, all-leather outfits. Some of the suedes were draped as skillfully as satin or silk, flexible and clinging. The leathers were of colors Lauren had not known could be secured on such material: pastels, cream, ivory, a dozen shades of purple, green, gold, and silver. The pièce de résistance was a black full suit, supple and soft as velvet, worn with a beret of the same black leather and half boots, on the heel of one of which was a silver spur. This outfit brought a standing ovation.

Mike grinned down at Lauren. "Had enough?"

As they slipped out, he asked, "Spying on the competition?"

Lauren laughed. "I'd like to know who prepares the leather for him. It's a well-guarded secret," she said with a smile. Then, soberly, she added, "All the designers attend or have their assistants at every show. Usually it's done fairly discreetly—"

"Snooping," Mike said. "As you were doing?"

"Are you a dress designer, Mike?" At his look of surprise, she added, "You were snooping too."

"I *was* hanging around on the off chance of meeting you," Mike explained almost too glibly. "I want to buy you a drink. I want to know all about you, Lauren Rose." He was not smiling now, but staring as though he wanted to pierce her lovely facade to discover the real woman beneath.

Lauren found herself telling him about her life before her marriage at nineteen to the brisk, worldly Al. He had projected a successful, man-of-the-world charisma that quite delighted Lauren's parents, who feared and despised all the youthful protesters, the laid-back drug cultists, and the flower children. To their ultraconservative minds, Allen Rose seemed a mature and sensible man who would protect their only child and guide her into a proper level of society. The glamour had lasted, for Lauren, about two years. From then on, it had been a matter of living according to the standards her parents had trained her to accept.

Of course Lauren did not tell Mike the sordid details, or even very much at all about her marriage, but he seemed to be able to read between the lines. He sat back in the booth he had chosen for them, relaxed and plainly interested, supplying a quiet question occasionally and unobtrusively signaling the steward for a drink from time to time.

Lauren was startled to find herself beginning on a third piña colada. She looked quickly up into Mike's face. He read her expression correctly and grinned.

"It's only your third," he excused her.

"Third! Ye gods, I never drink more than one."

"What, never?" he quoted, singing the correct notes.

"No, never," Lauren sang.

And then to finish the comic song from *H.M.S. Pinafore*, she and Mike chorused together, "Well, hardly ever!"

They shared a smile for their mutual addiction to Gilbert and Sullivan. "I would have bet you were a fan of the Savoyards," Mike said. "How many times have you seen *The Mikado*?"

"I'll tell you when you tell me how many times you've seen *The Pirates of Penzance*," Lauren challenged.

"You're not going to tell me you saw the original performance?" teased Mike. "Late 1870s, wasn't it?"

Lauren slanted him a look from under her long eyelashes. "Yes. Don't I wear my years well?"

"Wait till you get enough of them to boast about," Mike teased. "You're in the flowering time," he said with a grin, "like, fresh as a daisy? Saucy as a buttercup?"

"Stop right there, buster," Lauren advised, grinning back at him. "What about you? I've told you everything but my social security number! What do you do for a living?"

"I told you," Mike said succinctly. "I'm a talent scout for some of the bigger chains. I'm one of the people you can expect an offer from, after your show—if it's any good."

Lauren laughed aloud at his cheek. It was surprising how truly vital and happy he made her feel. She could never recall experiencing this lift of spirits, this true happiness, with any man before. She thought about his challenge for a minute. "My show is better than what you saw today, and a lot different. But you'll just have to wait, won't you?" She got up from the comfortable banquette. "Now I'm going to gloat over my new collection. See you later." She had to get away from him before she succumbed completely to his charm, that warm, vital maleness that was doing odd things to her senses.

"How about dinner tonight?" Mike had risen with

her. He held out his hand to assist her from the booth. Did he know how attractive he was?

Lauren smiled. "Your restaurant or mine?"

He recognized her search for information. "I was thinking, in my suite. More private. I'll call for you about eight."

Lauren shook her head. "It's the Maartens show tonight, and I want to see it. He's British, based in New York. Best of both cultures. Chic and understated."

"I still don't want to see it." Mike grinned. "Let's eat afterward. I'll pick you up outside the Royal Court Lounge after the show."

He was walking with her away from the lounge, his arm at her back. She could feel the warmth of it through the silk of her jump suit. Why was she so reluctant to let him go? She'd never had such difficulty saying good-bye to any man.

He seemed to understand her reluctance, and to share it. "Once around the deck?" he suggested. "To walk off those piña coladas?"

She accepted the offer. As they strolled along near the rail, Mike asked with an apparent lack of interest, "Will you be seeing much of your little friend?"

"You mean my model Dani? The one who tried to mistake you for the captain when we were embarking?"

"No, I mean the little teenager you were advising at breakfast."

"Gala Devine? No, I don't plan to. She's one of Carlos's models, as you guessed."

"What sort of costume would you suggest for a girl like Gala? Something like that very pretty jump suit you have on?"

"No. This is the wrong color for her, the wrong line for her extreme slenderness. She would look like a boy in it. Of course, she might want that effect."

"You don't look boyish," Mike answered.

"This suit is effective for my height, weight distribution, coloring, and age," Lauren explained. Rather than feeling complimented, Lauren felt he was mocking her, even testing her. She continued in a cold, matter-of-fact voice. "I try to design a dress with the woman who is likely to· wear it in my mind. A very plump woman, for instance, would look absurd in this. Or a very thin one."

Mike nodded.

Lauren, very much aware that the moment was spoiled, nodded back and walked swiftly away.

Unfortunately for her ruffled poise, she found Herbert Masen in her sitting room talking to Nella, who was dressed in a very fetching negligée from the new collection. Since she didn't particularly like Herbert and was wary of him after his horror stories about ships at sea, Nella must have put on the robe for the British doctor's delectation. Lauren set her lips firmly. It was her practice never to reprimand her models in front of outsiders; she said nothing, but her displeased glance at the robe got her point across to Nella.

"I was . . . waiting for the doctor to call," she explained, self-consciously. "When Mr. Masen knocked, I thought he was him."

"Better get back to bed, Nella. That robe isn't really warm enough for a sick woman," Lauren said a little waspishly. When the model had gone, Lauren turned to Herbert. "What can I do for you?" she asked shortly.

Herbert essayed his wheedling smile. "I wanted to apologize for coming in here drunk last night to wait for you, Laurie. I guess I just got worried when things seemed to be falling apart on you."

"How were you proposing to help me?" Lauren countered.

"Well," he said with a wide grin, "I was going to offer you my shoulder to cry on, as I remember."

"But you really don't remember," added Lauren. "You came on strong and nasty."

"Ah, forget that, babe," Herbert coaxed. "You know I've got your best interests at heart."

"So what else besides a shoulder did you have in mind?"

"I was going to propose to you again," he confessed, looking like a small boy. "You need a husband, Laurie baby. I can help you with the business details Al always saw to. Leave you free to do your thing with the designs."

Lauren studied the self-indulgent face of her husband's best friend. "Sorry, Herbert," she said as gently as she could. "I really don't need a husband right now."

"But you do need someone to get this show on the road—or off the deck. From the look of Nella and from what I hear about Dani, you haven't *got* a show. Be reasonable, Laurie-baby. You need me."

Where had Herbert dredged up this "Laurie-baby" bit? He sounded like an old-style Hollywood producer. Lauren was suddenly very tired of his fat, flabby face, body, and mind.

"You'll be glad to know that I'm handling it, Herbert," she said coolly. "Not to worry—" She caught herself short. Would that British phrase give Herbert a lead to her group of dancers? She didn't think so, but she didn't want to take any chances. Herbert was looking extremely curious, and he had no scruples about prying. "Look, Herbie-baby, I've got to get changed for tonight's show. It's Maartens, and he always has elegance."

"Have dinner with me, Lauren," Herbert wheedled. "I'm in the Princess Grill Restaurant. It's really something. I can have a guest if I work it right."

"I'm dieting, Herbert. See you later." She hustled

him, still talking, out the door and locked it. Then, poking her head into the models' bedroom, she said clearly, "Don't open that door for anyone but the doctor, got it? I don't want my new collection made available for anyone who wants to look at it."

That harsh but deserved rebuke quite crushed Nella.

Grimly, Lauren ordered a salad and tea to be delivered in one hour, and went to take a shower.

She wore an understated evening gown for the Maartens show. It was deep cream velvet, cut to look simple, a narrow sheath with a slit up one side and a slashed neckline front and back whose narrow opening reached almost to her waist. It had no ornament, depending upon purity of line and suppleness of material for its attractiveness. Her hair she dressed in a knot on top of her head, exposing her long, delicate throat and highlighting her face. She might not make a loud statement about her talents in this subtle gown, but she made a clear one. Shoes and bag of the cream velvet completed her ensemble. Fortified, Lauren went back up to the Royal Court Lounge and found her secluded position before most of the passengers arrived.

It was a much dressier group than that which had attended Janus's showing that afternoon. The women sparkled and flashed with jewels. There were bright and also deep rich colors. Lauren noted a number of taffeta dresses, and silently condoled the wearers who would emerge from nearly two hours' sitting down in a cramped space looking crumpled and squashed.

The show began exactly on time and proceeded with the smooth suavity of all Maartens' productions. The audience, much more restrained than the Janus admirers, murmured politely and applauded with gloved hands. Just before the final number—evening gowns and coats—Maartens himself appeared. He introduced the cruise director, Maida Hass, who announced the selection of judges. These were requested to stand upon the mention of their names. There were two women and one man. The first woman was Lady Winston-Bell. Quite a susurrus followed the announcement of her name, and a polite round of applause greeted her as she stood. The second woman was Mrs. Claire Lexington Cornelius, a socialite and respected member of an old New York clan. The applause was a little louder for her; she was well-known to any American with social ambitions. The man was rather a surprise.

"Our third judge is the New York columnist Mr. Rebel Crowell," said Maida Hass. There was a gasp and then applause. A slender, gray-haired man with wise dark-brown eyes rose and waved nonchalantly, acknowledging the response.

"This way, our show is sure to get superior coverage," teased Miss Hass. "Will it be *Time, Newsweek?*"

"Or *Playboy?*" yelled some wag in the crowd.

There was general laughter as the music started again, softly, for the final section of Maartens' showing.

While the audience were still applauding, Lauren slipped out of the lounge and found herself almost in Mike's arms. He wasted no time, leading her off rapidly to an elevator that took them up to the palatial suites which were the pride of the *QE II*.

Inside the spacious sitting room, Lauren stared around her with wide eyes. "So this is how the upper crust manages to scrape along?" she breathed. "Don't you feel a little cramped?"

Mike grinned. "If I am, I can always go out on my private balcony, or into one of my two bathrooms, or my—excuse it—bedroom. Want to see?" he teased.

"But of course," said Lauren, enthusiastically.

That seemed to surprise him. He stared at her, one

eyebrow lifted in a quizzical gesture that had her heart pounding.

"It's probably the only chance I'll ever have to see one of the super suites on the *Queen Elizabeth*," she explained. "Lead on, McDuff!"

"I believe that's *'Lay on, McDuff! And damn'd be him that first cries, 'Hold, enough!'*'" quoted Mike with the wickedest grin Lauren had ever seen. "Which of us is going to cry—"

"Me, right now," Lauren warned. "I'm starving, in case you've forgotten you invited me to dinner."

"Oh, all right," Mike grumbled. "Food! That's all you models think of. You can take the grand tour after dinner."

As though on signal, a steward brought in a cart set with tempting hors d'oeuvres and wine. Deftly he set out two plates on a small table near the open terrace doors. Lighting the candles, he rolled the cart beside the table so Mike and his guest could make their own choices. On the lower shelf, the cart held covered dishes set on warmers bearing the fish and vegetables for their second course. Murmuring that he would return with the rest of the meal when the gentleman rang, the steward slipped away.

Lauren surveyed the hors d'oeuvres with delight. "I may never get beyond this course," she murmured, helping herself to artichokes, mushrooms, olives, cucumbers, and cold salmon and mayonnaise. "Do hurry," she begged Mike.

"You were planning on waiting for me?" her host asked with a smile. "I'd better put you out of your misery." He finished pouring their wine and filled his own plate.

For several minutes there was a contented silence as they did justice to the food. Lauren drew a deep breath of pleasure. "What's in the hot dishes?" she asked.

"Ready for it?"

"This first was so good that I'm not sure whether to have seconds on it or move on to the next gourmet's delight."

Sole amandine, limes, rice with mushrooms, and baby green peas were so tempting that Lauren reluctantly accepted a fresh plate filled carefully by her host. After a few blissful moments, Lauren raised her head and directed a sharp glance at the big man across the table. "I've just figured it out," she said.

Mike met her glance with a chuckle. "What bee is in your designer bonnet now?"

"All this fabulous food is merely the prelude to some skulduggery—" Against her will, her lips quirked in delight at his charm.

"Softening you up for the kill?" Mike suggested. "Now that's an idea. What did you have in mind? For my skulduggery, that is?"

Most annoyingly, Lauren found herself coloring under that wicked, knowing gaze. She decided it might be better to share her suspicions honestly, rather than let this creature make his embarrassing assumptions. "I had an idea you might be in cahoots with Carlos or one of the others to find out how I intended to deal with the loss of two-thirds of my modeling team." She caught his raised brow and explained. "While Nella's out, I can't take her place because I have to help Dani on and off with her costumes, get the proper accessories, keep it running backstage."

"That does seem to present a problem," Mike said. "What have you decided?"

She looked into his face, trying to read the motives behind his behavior. Could she trust him? Lauren hadn't had much to do with the business end of the boutique, but she wasn't naïve. Al had told her grim stories of broken faith and spying and outright piracy. But she wanted to trust Mike. He had a clear and steady glance. She made a decision.

"I've hired some new models."

Mike whistled. "That sounds simple enough the way you say it, but where did you find models on the *QE II*? Are they trained?"

Lauren chuckled. "Oh, brother, are they trained."

Studying her enthusiastic, delighted expression, Mike shook his head. "If you've recruited some trained models on this ship, lady, you're a better entrepreneur and talent scout than I am. Who are they?"

Lauren stopped smiling and regarded him soberly. "I have your word not to tell anyone? Not even Dani or Nella?"

"The provocative information shall not pass my lips," he promised.

Lauren considered him carefully for another minute, her eyes lingering on his well-cut mouth. "I've hired Derek Strange and his troupe of dancers."

Mike stopped eating and stared at her. For a long moment she met his gaze squarely. Only the delicate lift of her eyebrows gave evidence of her wish for his opinion.

He put down his fork, and his eyes narrowed. "No rules against it?" he asked.

"None. I was lucky. We've got a *plot* for the production that will not only display the wearability of my designs, but will, I really believe, capture the interest of a rather bored Thursday-afternoon audience," Lauren said quickly. Then, with a wide grin, she added, "Carlos will have kittens."

Mike threw his head back in a shout of laughter. He

poured wine into her glass and then raised his in salute. "Triumph to the troupe!"

Lauren drank deeply. It was chancy, but it really was the only way she could have gone. She explained a little of the background to Mike: Herbert's subversion of Nella, Dani's determined search for a wealthy companion. "It's because she's really very much afraid the show is doomed to fail," she said to excuse the model's behavior. "If my show is the disaster Herbert has convinced her it will be, she'll get part of the blame. Bad luck rubs off on everybody connected. I don't blame her."

"How will she fit in with the new recruits?"

"I think she'll be a good sport," said Lauren. "Better than if I'd hired real models and given them better billing than she has. This way, she's doing her thing and they're doing theirs."

"This," Mike said fervently, "I have got to see."

"You're invited," Lauren replied demurely.

Mike rang for the steward, and when the man came, pushing another cart on which steamed more covered dishes with enticing odors, Mike ordered champagne.

Eating her beef Wellington with broccoli, Lauren was startled to realize that she was, for the first time in years, completely happy. Nothing ecstatic or complicated—just a bubbling pulse of bright contentment that seemed to make each simple thing she sensed a special pleasure: the food, both in taste and texture, was a delight; the room was softly lighted and fresh with the sea air coming through the open door; the sound of soft music coming faintly to her ears was a civilized counterpart to the darkly abrasive voice of her companion—*her companion.*

Michael was her happiness. Lauren stared at him, absorbing the dark shining hair, the tanned face, the beautifully cut lips, the two grooves between his dark eyebrows, the shining silver-gray eyes ... And more: the scent of him, faint spice mastered by the musk of clean male flesh. What would it taste like, that firm, tanned skin? Lauren dragged her gaze away from her dinner partner and tried to concentrate on the food in front of her.

So absorbed was she in savoring her own reactions that Mike's deep-voiced comment startled her. "I like a woman who appreciates good food."

Her glance flew up to meet the amusement in his eyes.

"And other things," he added, holding her gaze with his.

Lauren's knife cut through the tender, flaky pastry around the beef, sliced the reddish-brown filet, and conveyed the bite to her mouth. Her eyes closed as she savored the mouthful.

Mike chuckled. "A lady with gusto."

"It's all your fault," Lauren mocked. "You feed me this stuff, I relish it."

"Want dessert?" he asked.

Smiling, Lauren shook her head.

Quickly Mike tossed off the rest of his champagne and rose. "I feel reckless. Let's go to the Players Club and gamble."

Lauren wiped her lips and rose to her feet. "You don't think I'm already risking enough with my spur-of-the-moment presentation?"

Mike shrugged. "Hard to say for sure until I've seen it, but I trust your judgment."

Lauren thought that of all the personal comments he had made that evening, she liked this last one best.

An hour later she was standing at Mike's shoulder. He had a large pile of chips in front of him and an admiring group around him who were trying to follow his lead. He turned to her. "Bored? I am. Can't I persuade you to try your luck?"

Lauren smiled up at him. "If you're willing to be seen in my company there, I'd like to try the slot machines."

"Big spender," he mocked, but he cashed in his chips and went with her to the double row of one-armed bandits. He handed her a plastic cup full of quarters. "Live a little!"

Chuckling, Lauren began to play the slot machine. Her first few tries were failures, then she got ten quarters at once.

Mike sighed elaborately. "I suppose that means we'll be here all night."

Her next two tries netted nothing. And then she pulled the handle, discs whirled, colors flashed, and a spate of quarters came clanging out.

"Jackpot!" Lauren crowed. She counted and found she'd won fifty dollars.

"Now what? Craps?" Mike teased.

"Now we get out of here," Lauren said. "When I make a profit like this, I don't throw it away."

"Just a miser at heart," Mike grumbled.

"Oh, I'm planning to pay you back what you staked me," Lauren said loftily. "Twenty quarters?" She insisted on handing them over one by one, hoping to embarrass her cocky host in front of a few grinning players. While she was packing the rest of her winnings into her handbag, Lauren glanced along the row of machines toward the casino tables. Herbert was standing at one table, his arm around a slender redhead in a sequined dress. The girl couldn't have been out of her teens, in spite of the dress and heavy makeup. And standing behind the stool of a silver-haired man at the blackjack table, both hands on his shoulders, was Dani. She too seemed to be watching Herbert. Lauren didn't try to catch her attention.

Mike walked Lauren toward her section of the ship. He halted near one of the doors leading out on deck. "It's a beautiful night," he said softly. "Why don't we walk a little, to calm down your wild elation over your win?"

Lauren knew she didn't want the evening to end. It was good to be in the company of an attractive man, a man who seemed to be enjoying her as much as she enjoyed him.

"I'd like that," she said, and put her hand in the crook of the arm he offered. Under the smooth cloth of his jacket, she could feel his warm flesh, his hard muscles, and she thought of the bronzed body she'd first seen at the swimming pool.

It was beautiful on deck. The moon had gone down, but the warm darkness was filled with stars, both in the sky and reflected on the mirror-smooth sea. There were few people taking advantage of the deck, however. Most of the die-hards were probably in one or other of the nightclubs.

Mike leaned over and whispered in her ear. "Would you care to dance? We could go in—"

"Oh, no. This is perfect." Lauren said.

He made no comment, either romantic or sarcastic. He merely held her arm a little closer to his side and continued their stroll. After they had walked for a while, they moved to stand by the rail. Watching the silver-white foam churned up by the propellers, they became conscious of music filling the air. It was a waltz. Mike turned as though it were the most natural thing in the world and held out his arms to Lauren. She moved into them with equal unselfconsciousness. They danced dreamily over the deck, keeping within a small area, bodies controlled by the melody.

The music stopped. There was a sound of distant clapping.

"That was the home waltz," Mike said softly. He still kept her in his arms. He bent his head to her face. Lauren lifted her lips.

Loud voices impinged upon the magic serenity of the moment. Mike lifted his head with a low groan of disgust. " 'And only man is vile,' " he quoted.

"I'm glad you're not a chauvinist," Lauren said unsteadily. "One of those loud voices is definitely a woman's."

His teeth flashed in a grin as he turned to survey the loud-mouthed intruders, now advancing along the deck toward them.

"It's your would-be husband," he informed Lauren in a low voice. "Shall we leave?"

"Yes." Lauren had recognized Herbert's voice, and didn't want to meet him at the moment. Or have him find her with Mike.

"This way," directed Mike, hurrying her along the deck ahead of the quarreling duo. At that moment a door opened from the well-lighted lounge and several young people came out. The burst of light clearly revealed Lauren's petite figure. There was a shout from behind them.

"Lauren, I see you. Wait for me!" Herbert yelled.

Mike pulled her inside the door and closed it quickly. Then he led her almost at a run along a corridor, around a corner, and into an elevator.

"Which floor?" he asked.

When they got out, Mike walked Lauren to her suite. At the door, she stopped and turned to him. "That was a wonderful evening. Thank you," she said warmly.

Mike took her hand. "Going to ask me in for a nightcap?"

"Not tonight, Mike. Anything would be an anticlimax after that champagne!"

"Even this?" he asked, bending and placing his lips over hers. Lauren opened her mouth to comment and found herself relishing the pressure and warmth and flavor of his kiss. She tried to tell herself that she was enjoying the faintly moist sweetness of his mouth, nothing more. And then he moved forward and she found herself pressed against the door by the urgent authority of his body, and she was conscious of the whole man in a lightning thrill of tension and response. . . .

When he raised his head and stepped back, Lauren was dizzy. She tried to smile nonchalantly, but the glinting look in his eyes told her he was not deceived.

"Thank *you*," he said quietly.

She watched his broad shoulders moving off down the corridor. Once he passed directly under a ceiling light, and his dark hair gleamed for a moment. She fumbled for her key amid the packed mass of quarters and opened the door.

Chapter Three

Coming back to her suite after an early-morning swim, which had been disappointing because Mike wasn't there, Lauren opened the door to the sitting room and found Dani dressed and waiting for her.

"I thought I'd have breakfast with you, Ms. Rose," the model explained. "We need to talk."

"Give me ten minutes to get dressed, Dani," Lauren agreed.

She was ready in fifteen minutes, having decided to take time to wash and blow-dry her hair. She wore a short, pale-green top with matching slacks and tied a white silk scarf around her neck. Dani eyed her curiously.

"You always manage to look smart without cluttering up," she said, vaguely discontented with her own rather busy outfit. She had added bangles, six rings, and a gold chain belt to what had been planned as a basically simple gold cotton dress. Seeing Lauren eye her jewelry, Dani grimaced and stripped off the bangles and all but one of the rings.

"Better," Lauren approved.

"Let's go," Dani urged.

The model began to speak in a low tone as soon as they were seated at their usual table. The other places were empty, as the dance troupe seldom attended first sitting. "I wanted to tell you I'm sorry I haven't been more help to you so far, Ms. Rose," Dani began. "I guess, knowing that the show wouldn't be very good—"

"Hold it." Lauren smiled. "Who says our show isn't going to be any good?"

Dani frowned. "Well, it can't be, can it? Nella's out, and I can't wear all the clothes. Mr. Masen says—"

"Oh." Lauren nodded. "Herbert Masen told you we'd make a mess of things. You shouldn't listen to him."

Dani couldn't meet her eyes. "I don't like the guy, you know that. But he bought me a drink yesterday and explained very carefully that you'd more or less given up on the show and would marry him when you got back to Los Angeles." She looked embarrassed. "Are you really going to marry him, Ms. Rose?"

"That is one thing you can be sure of, Dani," Lauren said briskly. "I am *not* going to marry Herbert Masen."

"Well, I'm glad. He's a nerd." Dani perused the menu crossly. She always seemed enraged that she had to stick with the diet that ensured her model's thinness.

Lauren herself wasn't very hungry.

While they sipped grapefruit juice, Dani said with an attempt at brightness, "You'll want a rehearsal before Thursday, Ms. Rose. We'll have to—uh—synchronize our movements if there's just the two of us to handle the show."

Lauren debated whether to tell Dani about the radical change of plan. The girl was honest and fairly loyal, but she had an unguarded tongue, which might easily wag in the wrong quarters. While Lauren was considering how much to tell, the model glanced around the table.

"What happened to those actors or dancers or whatever they were? Did they get a different table?"

"I think they prefer to eat a little later," Lauren said vaguely.

"Where does Mr. Masen eat? I'm surprised he doesn't sit with you, if he thinks you're going to get married."

"Herbert prefers to eat in one of the more elegant dining rooms. I've never seen him in here."

"I saw him last night, in the casino. He had his arm around a girl young enough to be his daughter. I'm glad you're not going to marry that old creep. At *his* age, you'd think he'd have more sense."

"Don't be too harsh on Herbert. It's not easy to picture yourself worn out, of no more value."

Dani's shudder was sincere. Her large eyes glazed with fear that was very personal.

"Don't worry, Dani," her employer advised her. "You're at the top of your profession. A good show on board the *QE II* will send your ratings up."

"Then we've got to make sure this one's good," Dani vowed. "When do we rehearse?"

Lauren made up her mind. "Tomorrow morning, Dani. We'll go right after breakfast." She would check with Derek today, make sure he had things in hand, explain about the model's sensitivity and how she must be made to feel important in order to do her best work. She was sure the Stranges and their group could handle one temperamental model. In fact, she'd like to seek them out right now and see how the choreography was coming along. She set out happily from the Tables of the World Restaurant, leaving Dani to finish her Sanka and the last sweet roll.

Herbert was waiting for her outside the restaurant, glaring.

Lauren beat him to the punch. "So, you're living it up, Herbert. That was a very pretty child you had on your arm last night."

Herbert looked at her sourly. "Why didn't you stop when I called you?"

Lauren laughed.

Herbert's face got redder. "I looked for you at dinner, and at the Maartens show. Where were you?"

"Minding," Lauren said clearly, "my own business. You should try it sometime, Masen."

"Then you'd better watch that honcho you were running with," he snapped. "That's what I was trying to tell you last night. The guy's taking you for a ride."

"Why should he? What have I got that he wants?" Lauren prodded. If Herbert knew something, she'd better find out what it was.

Herbert was giving her his nasty smile. "Well, I don't suppose he'd mind a roll in the hay. But you don't even know who the guy is, or what he does for a living—if anything."

"His name is Michael, and he's a talent scout." It did seem rather bare, Lauren thought gloomily.

"Never heard of him," said Herbert. "If he's not a crook, he's some cheap gigolo living off foolish women—"

"Then he must have been doing good business lately," Lauren retorted. "I had the best dinner I've ever tasted in his suite last night. And you could have put my sitting room into one of his bathrooms."

"You had dinner in his suite?" Herbert's eyes narrowed to slits. "What's between you two? Making out on deck for anyone who walked past to see—"

Lauren wasn't going to make any excuses to Al's old friend. "It really isn't your business, is it? Why don't you buzz off?"

Now the mask of hearty, close friendship slipped completely from Herbert's pudgy features and his eyes and voice were colder than Al's had ever been as he said, "It sure as hell is my business, *baby*. I've got shares in the boutique and I'm not standing still while some cheap crook robs us blind."

"Shares," Lauren sneered. "See my lawyer when you get back to Los Angeles. I'll buy you out." Relishing the pure shock on his face, she added, "The next time you're in partnership with anybody, watch your drinking. You spilled everything you knew about me and the business to that same Michael you're bad-mouthing now."

She walked away, leaving the man staring after her with an empty look.

Her session with the troupe restored her faith. They were wonderful. Fresh and lively and more graceful than any men had a right to be, Derek and Tony mimed their admiration for the cleaning women in the gorgeous gowns. Even better, the display dances Tony had choreographed would show Lauren's designs in luscious, flowing detail.

"I love it!" she breathed.

The troupe laughed. "You're a real hard sell, Mrs. Rose." Tony grinned. "I thought you'd have *some* criticism?"

"I have. You ought to be doing this on a real stage, before a real audience, not just for a fashion show."

"But what a fashion show." Violet laughed. "I can hardly wait to see the rest of your competition, so I'll be sure how much better you are. And those audiences aren't your run-of-the-mill folks. They're pace-setters. Oh, we'll get recognition."

Lauren went to lunch with a lighter heart. They wouldn't let her down: she mustn't fail them. At the table, she met a frantic Dani.

"What's wrong? Is Nella sick?"

Dani grimaced. "She's in love, which is worse. I can't stand her constant cooing. She's having lunch with her doctor, so I thought I'd better clue you in—"

"I'm not worried about her crush on the handsome

Britisher." Lauren smiled. "I prefer cooing to whining any day."

"I don't mean about Nella. I'm talking about Herbert and that beef-cake you've been palsy with. You know, Mike."

"What about Mike?" Lauren's mouth felt dry and she sipped some water and stared at the menu.

"Just that I saw him with old Herbert not fifteen minutes ago in the corner of the Crown and Anchor. I was just looking for a friend, and I saw them. They had their heads close like they didn't want anybody to hear what they were saying." She glanced at Lauren shrewdly. "I thought you'd better know."

Lauren drew in a steadying breath. "Well, unless Herbert's won an Academy Award for acting recently, they really aren't buddies. He's just been giving me the third-degree for daring to have dinner with Mike last night. Claims he's either a gigolo or a crook."

"Since when would either of those professions put Masen off?" Dani asked. "It looked like he was trying to make a deal with the guy. Watch it, Ms. Rose."

Rather gloomily Lauren thanked the model for her concern and then told her, with grim threats if she even breathed a word to anybody on the ship, about the dance production.

As she had feared, Dani was at first a little prickly about her own importance and position in the show. After Lauren had explained it in painstaking detail, however, Dani brightened.

"It might be fun at that," she said, obviously thinking of the several times she would be lifted and carried around by two handsome men. "You're sure the dancing part of it won't make me look silly?"

"Dani, you'll be showcased like never before," Lauren

promised. "Come on and meet them and we'll prove it."

The women went quickly to the reserved room and Lauren gave the agreed-upon knock. Tony let them in and gave Dani his best smile. The troupe clustered around her and told her how much they would enjoy working with a professional model. Then Violet played and the rest demonstrated their routines.

Dani loved it. "We're going to be the hit of the trip," she bubbled. "It's like a musical comedy."

"Remember you promised not to breathe a word," Lauren cautioned. "Herbert Masen will find a way to wreck us if he finds out."

She left Dani working with the group and went to discuss her music with Maida Hass. There was a small orchestra who regularly played for all the showings. Violet had given her the exact score the dancers required. It wasn't difficult music, but the timing was all-important.

The leader of the musicians, a lanky young man with dreams of glory with one of the great symphony orchestras, was at first a little condescending about Tony's choices. Lauren fixed him with a stern, business-like eye.

"Poor or badly timed playing can ruin a show," she said quietly. "If you don't think you'll feel comfortable with this, let me know now and I'll find someone who can handle it."

"We can handle it," the youth hurried to say. "Will there be a rehearsal? The other designers rehearse in the mornings."

Lauren had forgotten that part of it. She couldn't expose her idea out here in the lounge, where any passerby could watch. "Have you got free time tomorrow morning?"

"Yes," he said, consulting a clipboard. "Ten to eleven."

"Please be in the smaller gym—the old one—at ten, will you?" She smiled at the musicians. "Thank you all."

And Heaven help us if they talk, she thought. It was becoming harder every minute to keep a secret on the great ship. She could only hope that her failure to rehearse her one model in the lounge would convince her ill-wishers that she didn't have a show.

She didn't see Mike at the afternoon showing. Ben Nowak did his usual very popular presentation with a bevy of young men and women models. He had the runway enlarged by the addition of a wide crosspiece near the far end, where his youthful mannequins did their college and high-school antics. Very few of the first-class passengers attended; Nowak, already a multimillionaire, couldn't care less. Lauren left the show feeling reassured; although the background music was bright and modern, there was no real dancing, no threat to her show.

She wasn't worried about Adah Shere that night, either. Shere was a lovely Hindu woman, whose signature was the gold-and-silver decorated saris she wore. Her creations were always Oriental in some particular way, either by the line of the costume or by the materials or embroidery. It was a lovely look, but not all women could carry it off. Some of her most enthusiastic and devoted clients were film and theater stars and a few wealthy patronesses of the arts, especially ballet. The audience tonight would be almost entirely made up of first-class passengers, but it would be a buyers' group, well worth the effort.

Lauren carefully chose her costume for this showing. Some of Adah Shere's clients might well find her own designs appealing. After all, they couldn't dress like Chinese empresses and Indian temple dancers all the time. She chose a figure-caressing, low-cut top of pastel sequins, set on a slim, pale-green full-length skirt with a slit up the back as far as her knees. Over this was a caftan of sheerest chiffon, with long, loose sleeves. This was in the same pale green. The only ornament was a flat sequin collar three inches wide, which curved around the neck and hooked discreetly at the front. As she moved, the shimmering sequins moved sensuously with her torso under the delicate chiffon.

Lauren loved it. She wished that Mike were escorting her to the showing. In hopes of seeing him, she made up with particular care in her softest colors and let her shining hair fall naturally to her shoulders.

The first person she saw as she slipped into the lounge was Mike. He was with a beautiful brunette in black lace and diamonds. They were sitting with the audience. Mike looked splendid in white tie and tails. Several other successful and prominent-looking men and women sat next to them and chatted back and forth while they waited for the showing.

Lauren made her way quietly to a chair near the end of the runway. She couldn't lurk on the couch tonight, not in this gown. Holding her head high, she walked to her seat. She kept her eyes away from the seats occupied by Mike and his party, but her thoughts were busy. Entrepreneur—talent scout, he had said. Obviously operating on a high level. What kind of talent? Was the gorgeous brunette a movie star or an actress? Did Mike have a special relationship with her? Lauren was telling herself to forget it and concentrate on the show as the lights dimmed for the first announcements and commentary.

Someone slid into the empty chair next to Lauren.

Startled, she turned, half-expecting to see Mike.

It was Tony, looking very British and elegantly lean

in formal evening gear. "You look beautiful," he murmured in her ear. "Like the sultan's dream." He mimed a devilish leer.

Lauren found herself chuckling.

The showing was a great success. Most of the costumes were special, one-wearing-and-then-lay-away-for-your-children items. This year Adah Shere had gone into metallic and jewel-encrusted braids on heavy brocades that were themselves woven with gold and silver. It was a stunning presentation . . . for the very wealthy. The audience loved it.

During the interval, Lauren quizzed Tony as to his reason for appearing. "Is there a problem? I've got a music rehearsal for you in the gym tomorrow morning from ten till eleven. Okay?"

"Excellent," Tony agreed. "We need Vi for the show; can't let her keep tinkling away on the piano."

His good spirits restored Lauren's pleasant mood. She *was* here on board the greatest luxury ship afloat to show her designs, wasn't she? Not to worry about quarrels with Herbert Masen or the real motives of mysterious strangers. However attractive they were.

She smiled at Tony. "Can I treat you to a sherry at the pub?"

He grinned with her at her attempt at an English accent. "That speech calls for an 'old boy?' at the end of it. Thanks, but we're all going up to one of the nightclubs as a treat for working so hard. I really came down to ask if you cared to join us."

"No, thanks. I think I'll just check on Nella. I've left her alone so far."

Tony expressed his regrets and escorted her out of the lounge before he left to pick up his crowd. Lauren hadn't much desire to go single to any of the other lounges or bars, but she felt too restless to return to her room so early. Recalling her success at the slot machines, she wandered to the casino. The sight of Herbert with his young girl sent her in the other direction. She was approaching her own suite when a dark figure approached her suddenly from around a corner.

"Taxi, lady?" Mike murmured, grinning.

"Did you drop your other fare or did she drop you?" Lauren taunted.

"Jealous?" asked the insufferable man.

"Yes," Lauren admitted.

His eyebrows, those heavy, masterful dark weapons, rose. In a very different voice—his deep, softly abrasive tone that thrilled along Lauren's nerves—he said, "Can I believe that, Mrs. Rose?"

Lauren faced his challenging eyes.

"Do you want to?"

He moved forward and took her arm in one of his large hands. "Come up to my suite and we'll discuss it."

"Let's walk on deck," Lauren counterproposed. She was just a little nervous now of her own daring.

Mike grinned. "It's raining hard. Come on."

Lauren went.

The sitting room was softly lighted. Music played from an unseen tape or radio. There were flowers in bowls, diffusing their delicate sweetness, and against the closed french doors to the balcony rain pounded heavily. Mike waved his hand at it.

"Special order. I spoke to Neptune."

"You really wanted me to come here tonight?" Lauren asked. Her voice wasn't as confidently flip as she'd intended.

"I really did," he avowed. "I had an appointment I couldn't get out of, for dinner and the Shere showing. When I ditched that crowd, I went right to your suite." He moved over and took Lauren into his arms. For a long moment he held her away from him, hands hard on her upper arms, as he scrutinized the costume and the woman in it.

"I think I'd have known that was September Song even if you weren't wearing it," he said at last. "It's feminine, gentle, lovely. It suits you."

Lauren couldn't take her eyes off his face as it bent down over hers. When the beautifully cut, sensuous lips were so close to hers that she could feel the warmth of his breath, she slowly lowered her eyelids.

The dark voice said softly, "Look at me, Lauren. I want to see your violet eyes when I kiss you."

Almost drowsily, she lifted her lids and he kissed her. It was a slow, easy, gentle kiss. A *friendly* kiss, Lauren thought, alarmed at her own disappointment. Still, it had magic, a slow, sensuous stroking of his firm lips against hers. Lauren gave herself up to it. Even if it lacked the passionate demand she had been hoping for, it was richly caressing and comforting. When she felt herself fully relaxed, melted into his arms, Mike removed his lips with a slow regret that communicated itself to her.

"First we'll have a drink and a snack. I couldn't eat any dinner, worrying about what you were doing."

Lauren walked over and sat down on a comfortable lounge chair. "I forgot to eat tonight," she confessed. "I was trying to look my best for Shere's presentation."

"You succeeded." He was bringing a chilled bottle and a large, covered silver dish from the refrigerator in the guest bathroom. "Sandwiches," he boasted happily. "The British do them so well, ever since good old Lord Sandwich invented the bally things."

Chuckling, Lauren agreed. She took off the cover while Mike poured the wine into glasses. The sandwiches looked so good that she couldn't wait. She was biting into a chicken with mayonnaise as Mike turned around.

"Caught you! Trying to steal a march, are you? You'll pay for that, my girl."

Lauren found herself choking with laughter. Mike offered her a glass of chilled wine. Sipping it, she regarded him with laughter-filled eyes.

He returned the compliment. "Fun, eh?"

Lauren nodded at him. "I haven't felt this relaxed in a long time," she admitted honestly. "You know the script in business: life is real, life is earnest, and the cash flow is our only goal."

"But you're on the creative end," Mike admonished. "That ought to ease some pressures, surely?"

"My husband's been dead for several years," said Lauren quietly. "I'm trying—with the help of a fabulous accountant, who is both loyal and competent—to run the whole thing myself."

Mike tipped his dark head to one side, scanning her face. "Wouldn't it make sense to sign up with one of the big corporations, let them handle the commercial end of it?"

"I'd have to make sure none of my own staff were fired," mused Lauren, her expression telling the man that she was indeed considering the idea of a contract.

"Why don't you let me handle it for you?" he said. "It's my field, after all. And your own lawyer could check the proposition carefully."

"Have you direct affiliations with any special company, Mike, or do you act as a middleman only?"

"I've got a lead to Landrill's," he told her. "But that's not my only field. I work with an international hotel chain, scouting interesting sites for new buildings and talented young executives—both male and female—to run them with class and good business sense."

Lauren chuckled. "So you're not a male chauvinist. And from the sound of it, you've got an exciting job. I guess you've been told, if you work with Landrill's, that they've already made September Song an offer?"

"*One?* Lady, they tried four times to set up a deal with your husband. They *believe* in you, Mrs. Rose."

"At least they believe I can make them a bundle," she retorted.

"Why not? Aren't you in designing to make money? You don't give away the dresses," he challenged a little harshly.

Lauren nodded. She understood the reason for his annoyance. Of course, she was in the business of designing to make money. Sometimes the sheer pleasure of seeing one of her ideas come alive was more than enough payment for hours of work and frequent frustration, but if it were not for the fact that women were willing to pay a good price for her dresses she wouldn't be able to enjoy her creative satisfactions. She faced Mike with an open smile.

"You're right, of course. We creative types should never forget that we don't design in a vacuum. Somebody has to want what we make."

"And Landrill's will make sure that lots of women know how attractive and flattering your line of clothing is. Can I put together a deal?"

Lauren nodded. This Fashion Cruise had opened her eyes; it would be increasingly difficult for her to do battle alone in the marketplace and keep up her creative work at the same time. She needed a manager; Al had kept all the business side of the operation away from her, so she really didn't know enough to cope, hadn't the skills or the toughness or the knowledge it took. She began to realize that she really didn't want to fight that battle. She wanted to design clothing. Was that too much to ask? She noticed that Mike was watching her, probably evaluating her changing expressions.

"Yes, let's see what your lawyer and mine can work out," she said.

His face showed only the normal pleasure at the successful conclusion of negotiations. "Now we've got that settled," he said, "let's eat, drink, and forget that tomorrow we diet."

The sandwiches were delicious: chicken breast, roast beef, cheese with bacon, pâté, even sliced tomatoes with pepper and mayonnaise. They fought over the last of that kind.

Lauren drank more wine than she usually allowed herself. As a result, her mood became more and more unguarded. After one particularly provocative remark from her, Mike phoned for coffee.

"I won't have you accusing me, tomorrow, of getting you—ah—mellow and then clinching a deal," he teased, eyes warmly satisfied.

Lauren felt the laughter fading from her lips as it struck her that she had thrown away her independence as lightly as she had eaten the sandwiches. "I wasn't too hard to persuade, was I?" she mocked herself.

Mike frowned. "I don't think I like the sound of that."

Lauren shrugged. "Dani tells me you and Herbert were having a heart-to-heart in the pub. Was he telling you where I am vulnerable? Or were you hiring him as a hotel manager?"

"I wouldn't hire Masen to pass out free samples," Mike snapped. "For your information, Mrs. Rose, *he* was telling *me* that you two had been lovers ever since your husband died." Ignoring Lauren's gasp of outrage, Mike went on. "When I reminded him that his behavior on this trip hadn't been exactly devoted, he said he was trying to make you jealous."

Lauren's outrage dissolved in surprised laughter. "Jealous?" she hooted. "Of Herbert?"

Mike grinned. "My reaction exactly. Too bad Dani didn't get close enough to hear what I replied to that statement."

Lauren got up and went to him. She met his quizzical glance squarely. "I'm sorry I said that about persuasion. Since I came on this trip, I've been forced to face the fact that I really *don't* know all the answers, either about my own profession or about other human beings. I don't know what's behind anyone's mask. I've let Herbert hang around and harass me; even Tony told me I was an easy sell when I agreed without criticism to his choreography. I guess the truth is I suddenly felt very . . . insecure." She put on a bright smile. "Would you say I'm out of my league?"

Mike put his arms around her and pulled her close. "I'd say you were a very honest, modest, intelligent human being who's fighting hard to produce an innovative presentation of her talent. With no help from people she could have expected it from. It's lucky you ran into those dancers and persuaded them to help you, but I think you would have found some way to handle it even if you hadn't. You're a fighter, Lauren."

She felt a light pressure on her hair. Was he kissing her? She turned her face up to meet his intent gaze. He was smiling down at her, a warm light in his silver eyes.

"You're pretty, too," he added.

He released her as the steward knocked and entered with their coffee. As she poured it, Lauren wanted to ask him what he thought of her. She had meant it when she told him she couldn't appraise people, couldn't read their motives or their intentions. She especially couldn't pigeonhole Mike. He wasn't like any man she'd ever met.

"I haven't really known many men," she said, not realizing how vulnerable she looked, small and exquisite and feminine in the corner of the huge sofa. "I never understood my father. I think I was afraid of him, although he never hurt me. He had very rigid views about the place of women, especially girl children, in his world. I know it's archaic, but I wouldn't have dared to disagree with any of his judgments, no matter how chauvinistic and unreasonable they were. I can't understand the way I felt." She sighed and shook her head. Mike didn't comment. He sat drinking his coffee and listening as she spoke.

Lauren went on. "Al asked my father before he asked me. My father was very wealthy and Al was just beginning to make his own way. Then Dad told me *I'd* made a good choice. Al knew how to present himself to older, conservative men. He was a man's man: loved hunting and fishing and drinking with other men. He wasn't ever really comfortable with a woman, except in bed. And then only briefly."

She heard herself making these embarrassingly blunt admissions but couldn't seem to stop. Mike was listening as though he really cared, as though it mattered to him what had happened to her and what she thought. It struck her that very few people had ever truly listened to what she had to say. Her father certainly never had. Her mother had listened but not understood. Al had never made a pretense of discussing anything with her beyond her next collection and the problems it might present to his sales campaign. Lauren sighed and relaxed against the back of the comfortable sofa. She smiled trustingly.

"Now you," she invited.

"Me?" Mike rose and placed his cup and saucer on the coffee table.

"Aren't you going to share with me?" All at once she felt like some sort of groupie in a therapy rap session.

Mike loomed over her, bent to seize her hands, and pulled her to her feet. She was so close to him that she felt the heat from his body.

"Yes, I'm going to share with you, Lauren Rose. I'm going to share the loneliness we both feel under our bright impersonal masks. And the hunger we have for the act of love with someone to whom it means more than lust— Oh, what's the use of words? Let me show you."

He lifted her easily and carried her into the bedroom. Putting her down gently beside the bed, he began to remove her clothing. His big hands were gentle at her throat as he unhooked the sequin collar, then took off the delicate, filmy caftan. At first Lauren couldn't face him, but her glance was finally drawn to his face as to a magnet. His expression was solemn, absorbed, and told Lauren he considered her important to him, valuable, even. As though what he was doing was a kind of worship. So when he gently took the dress from her body, Lauren felt no shame, only a faint sense of embarrassment that Mike might not find her worthy of his passionate regard.

When he had removed the last of her clothing, Mike lifted her gently onto the bed. Then he turned and walked to the door. Lauren voiced a small inarticulate cry. He turned at once.

"Just for our privacy," he said softly, closing and locking the door. Then he came back to the bed and began to strip. Lauren couldn't take her eyes from his body. She had seen it when they swam in the pool, big and brown and well-muscled, but this disrobing was a thousand times more erotic. He had draped her costume carefully over a chair; his own clothes he merely dropped to the floor. Then he came to stand beside her.

"May I leave the lights on, Lauren?" he asked. And when she would have objected, fearing that her body would disappoint him, he said, "Please, you are so lovely," and she could not deny him.

She held out her arms to him. With a sigh as deep as a groan, Mike came down beside her on the bed and took her into his arms.

She had never known such pleasure. He shared with her his delight in every part of her body. His lips and hands moved over her, sweetly tormenting and rousing her. Within a few minutes he had excited her in ways she had not known were possible. Her muscles tensed with the need to respond to him. Warmth flooded her, and she trembled involuntarily. When his hand moved over her body and down to her hips, Lauren sobbed, "Yes, Mike. Yes," and clung to him, holding him close to her.

Moving together, murmuring tenderness against each other's lips and shoulders and throats, they drove on to ecstasy together, reaching the exploding moment at the same quivering instant. Gasping, they relaxed against the soft bed, still close in each other's arms. Mike settled her more comfortably against him, pulling her head over onto his chest and holding it there.

Lauren began to laugh soundlessly. Mike felt her body's small tremors and lifted her chin so he could see her face. "What is it, sweetheart? Why are you laughing?" His smile was tender.

Lauren smiled into his eyes. "Your hair tickles my nose." She patted the curly black thatch on his chest with possessive fingers.

Mike pretended exasperation. "I give you world-class treatment and you say my hair tickles! I thought you were a romantic."

It was *comfortable* to share small jokes, Lauren decided; a sort of defense against the earth-shaking force of what they had shared. It gave that mindless, overwhelming physical ecstasy a warm, human individuality—made it truly *theirs*. She grinned. "That was world-class?" she teased.

It was Mike's turn to laugh, full-throatedly, his chest shaking her. "I see I have myself an insatiable female here." He chuckled, pulling her on top of him and pinning her to him. He began a tantalizing stroking, a sensual massage that brought her quickly to an ardent response.

Later, Lauren was roused from light slumber to find Mike stroking her hair gently. She looked up at him with drowsy eyes, recalling with wonder the strange, compelling wave of feeling that had caught them both up into an alluring rapture of physical delight that led to a piercing, almost agonized ecstasy. It had been a time removed from everyday reality, a moment when they were no longer Lauren and Mike, no longer even male and female, but instead a mindless centering of awareness, of sensation, which focused in their joined bodies. Lauren inhaled sharply at the memory.

"Mike," she said softly, smiling at the strong, beautiful face, relishing their shared delight. She yawned involuntarily, then stretched herself as gracefully as a cat, in the process moving her breast against him.

He bent his dark head to her, kissing her gently, reassuring her. Then he groaned as she pressed his head against the rounded flesh of her breast, stroking his neck and shoulders.

"It was unbelievable, wasn't it?" he whispered against

her flesh. "I have never known a woman who was so ardent, so able to love me and accept my lovemaking." He stroked her breast, then tantalized that tender flesh with sweet butterfly kisses.

Al had always turned away and gone to sleep as soon as he had satisfied himself, Lauren remembered. Never once had he shared his feelings, told her that he valued their lovemaking.

Seeing the lost look on her face, Mike gathered her closer to his body. His voice was uneven. "I didn't know it could be so . . ." He broke off with a groan. "I adore you."

Suddenly shy of this great sleek tiger, warm and virile against her body, Lauren drew away a little. "What time is it? I'd better go back to my stateroom now."

As she moved to get up, he caught her to him. "I won't let you go creeping back to your cabin in the middle of the night."

"Better than having half the crew see me returning in the daylight wearing an evening gown," Lauren said ruefully. "I'm not very skilled at intrigue."

Mike sat up quickly. "Intrigue? Is that what you call it? Madam, I shall not permit you to beat a clandestine retreat from my bedroom."

Lauren stared at the magnificent virility of him and felt her treacherous heart melt. If he really wished her to stay . . . It did seem a flat ending, a commonplace dawn, after a night of such shared joy.

"I can't stay here indefinitely," she protested, too weakly.

"Why not?" demanded Mike, the indulgent conqueror. "We can send for your toothbrush and you don't need a nightgown."

"Be serious," she begged with a laugh.

"Be yourself," he advised her coolly. "Lauren Rose,

the designer of September Song, design something! Make yourself a bathing suit out of a sheet or something, and come for a swim with me. After that, you can return to your cabin with perfect propriety."

It was easy to see he was accustomed to getting his own way with women. That idea introduced a host of disturbing pictures of Mike with a succession of beauties, taking them to swim in his spacious pool in his own home. Still, she refused to let jealousy spoil the wonderful experience they had shared. Go swimming? Make herself a suit? Why not? She began to smile. Her eyes sparkled.

"Have you got a pair of scissors?" she asked.

"I believe there's a sewing kit in the guest bathroom. Cunard thinks of everything."

Lauren was already in the bathroom. Her voice rang out, pleased and interested, "There are several extra towels and bath sheets. September Song is about to launch a terry-cloth trend."

Half an hour later, Lauren paraded into the sitting room and struck a pose. Mike, lounging in his trunks and robe, rose to applaud.

"You'd never get away with that any place but the Riviera or Black's Beach, but I think you look terrific. In fact, it gives me an idea—" He began a mock-predatory advance.

Lauren dodged past him, laughing. Her costume was fetching, but too fragile for a struggle. Two facecloths and two hand towels in rust, stitched together, paid token service to modesty. Lauren had also cut a T-slit in a rust-colored bath sheet, which she now donned as a poncho.

"On to the pool," she commanded. "Before half the ship is awake to review my latest design."

"You know that gorgeous creation you were wearing last night?"

"You mean the gown you removed so cavalierly?"

"I was careful," Mike protested. "I'll wrap it in a clothes bag and return it to your stateroom before dinner tonight, which, by the way, you will have with me."

"It's Carlos de Sevile's showing," Lauren said, at once sober as she contemplated the challenge. "I must attend."

"We'll eat here afterward," Mike said firmly. "I'm going to take you to the show. I can't let you go unguarded among the wolves."

Chapter Four

When she returned to her cabin, much refreshed after her swim, she found both Dani and Nella still sleeping. So much for her worry about gossip, Lauren thought. But she did not escape completely. A sullen Herbert waited for her outside the restaurant as she emerged after breakfast. He took her arm roughly.

"We're going to talk. In your sitting room."

"I'm busy this morning with the presentation for September Song."

"About time," Herbert sneered. "Your show is tomorrow afternoon and you haven't even rehearsed yet."

"How do you know I haven't rehearsed? Snooping?"

"Until and unless you buy my shares, I've got a legitimate right to know what's going on. When do you rehearse?"

"You aren't going to watch us," Lauren said grimly. "You've put Nella out of action—"

"She never was in it," he taunted. "What a crummy pair of old bats you chose for your models." He jerked at her arm. "Let's go down to your suite."

To avoid a scene, Lauren led the way. Her own bedroom door was locked, as she had left it after her swim, and the models' door was closed. Lauren indicated a chair. Herbert flounced into it.

"Well?" Lauren asked coolly.

"What's going on?" Herbert growled.

"I'm putting on a show tomorrow afternoon. I'm rehearsing for it today, in secret. Dani and Nella are going to be there, as of course am I. That's all you need to know."

"I'm going to see that rehearsal."

"Why?" Lauren's voice was cold. "You know nothing about staging a fashion show. You know nothing about fashions. You have never, even when Al was managing the boutique, had anything to do with the presentations. And I don't like the sabotaging you've been doing on this trip, or your lies. You've never been my lover and you never will be. Now leave me alone and leave the models alone, or I'll complain to the judges about your harassment."

Glaring at her, Herbert could see that she meant every word. He struggled to think of a reply, but clearly could not in the face of Lauren's open hostility. He got up from the chair and strode over to the door. Flinging it open, he said pompously, "You'll regret your high-handed behavior, Lauren. I tried to save your bacon, but you don't want my help. Al wouldn't be very proud of the kind of woman you've turned into." He stalked out, slamming the door after him.

Dani poked her head out of her bedroom. "Geez, he's awfully noisy for this early in the morning. What brought that on?"

"Get ready for the rehearsal," Lauren said harshly. "And if you breathe one word to that creep about the show, I'll push you overboard."

Dani grinned. "Attagirl, Ms. Rose! Give 'im hell."

The two women smiled at one another.

The ten-o'clock rehearsal went very well. The orchestra had taken time to familiarize themselves with Tony's score, and after a few rough spots were ironed out, the presentation sparkled. An extra bonus was the presence of Nella, who, urged by obscure guilt feelings even more than by her fear of losing her salary, insisted upon going with Lauren and Dani to the rehearsal. Lauren told her that if she ever breathed one word about the revamped show to any living being, she, Lauren, would personally make sure that Nella never modeled again in the United States. Nella believed her.

She was as enchanted with the dance and mime as Dani had been, and announced herself perfectly willing to model the suits and accessories, the sports wear and anything else that had been made for her. She agreed very happily to do her usual job in all the sections but the dance-mime, and to stay backstage to help the troupe with costume changes for that.

Lauren couldn't believe her ears. Nella restored to health was one thing; Nella willing to help backstage and to model her own costumes without fussing was even better. Lauren looked at her with a suspicious eye. "What's made the change?" she queried.

"Michael came by while you were at breakfast. He was returning the dress you'd sent to the cleaner-valet service. He says the tear is mended so neatly you'd never believe there had been one. Gee, he's nice. I didn't believe such a dishy guy would pick up our cleaning."

"Was that all he said?" Lauren asked as calmly as possible.

"No. He promised Dani and me a bonus if we did a good job. He explained how Mr. Masen's been trying to do us dirt. That's rotten."

Lauren and Dani exchanged glances. "A unanimous vote," murmured Lauren.

The three women ate lunch together and then went

on to the afternoon presentation. It was Telford of Boston, the preppy guru, and predictably conservative-nostalgic. The elite loved it, of course. Like Nowak's show and Janus's, it had its own cult of dedicated buyers. Lauren and her models, all elegantly dressed, drew a number of admiring glances as they took their seats, but no comments.

"You'd think they'd ask about the clothes," Nella grumbled, who was very proud of the way she looked in a rich amber silk cocktail dress that glorified her hair and her bosom:

"They think you're part of the audience," Dani quipped. "One of the Back Bay elite."

"Haven't you heard about Bostonians?" Lauren whispered. "They speak only to each other and God."

"Oh," Nella said, round-eyed and credulous. Dani grimaced.

"I've made arrangements for you both to have a session of massage, Jacuzzi, and facial at the Golden Door spa this afternoon," Lauren told them. "Then, tonight, we'll all go to Carlos de Sevile's showing. You'll wear your special evening gowns for that." She smiled at their brightening look. "I'll help you dress."

"Can we eat before the showing?" Nella asked. "I'm always starved."

"After," Lauren decided. "That way, we don't take a chance on spilling food on those clothes."

Dani and Nella laughed heartily. Lauren crossed her fingers and kept her mouth closed.

"Then tomorrow, at about eight A.M., Derek and Tony have scheduled a dress rehearsal, with costumes, music, the works. I'll get a steward to take the clothes racks to the old gym. We put on our September Song showing at two P.M. in the Royal Court Lounge. Think you can handle it?" she asked encouragingly.

Both models nodded.

"I suggest an early night tonight, in view of the eight-o'clock rehearsal."

Again the models nodded. Lauren smiled at them, feeling a real sense of gratitude to both. In spite of Herbert's efforts and Dani's roving eyes, they were rallying around Lauren. Her smile warmed.

"Thank you both," she said sincerely. "I really appreciate your help. I couldn't do it without you."

Nella beamed and Dani looked a little embarrassed.

Lauren said, "Enough schmaltz already. Off you go to the spa and live it up."

When they had disappeared, Lauren went to her suite. From there she phoned the purser's office and asked for a reliable steward to take the racks of costumes to the rehearsal by eight o'clock the following morning. This was promised, and with a feeling of relief Lauren hung up the phone. She sat on the couch, daydreaming, for a long moment. Mike was always there at the back of her mind, warm and concerned and subtly supportive. Lauren wondered why a man as attractive and serious as Mike hadn't been snapped up long ago. He'd never revealed anything about his private life, and not too much about his business interests. And, yet, surely he didn't hop into bed with a different woman every night. Last night had to be something special. Lauren knew it had been for her. Did Mike feel any sense of commitment? He had said he wouldn't let her go unguarded among the wolves, that he would escort her to the de Sevile showing and then bring her to his suite for dinner afterward.

Lauren stared ahead without seeing the pleasant furnishings of the suite. What did she feel about Mike? Last night had been something rare and wonderful, an evening out of time. She didn't regret one minute of it, although she was not a woman who took love or sex lightly. She had known only one man in her life until last night with Mike. Did she want to go on with him after the cruise? Did he want to commit himself to a serious relationship? And what would it be? An affair? Marriage? How could she tell, until Mike made his wishes known to her?

Lauren got up and walked restlessly about the small space. If Mike wanted a brief affair, would that be enough for her? Although she was very tolerant of such casual or even serious relationships among her friends and acquaintances, would she herself be happy in that kind of an association? With a sense of unease, Lauren felt that she would not. Yet, strangely, she did not begrudge the closeness, the loving sexual experience of the previous night. It had felt so *right*, so naturally sweet and satisfying. Had it been that way for Mike also? And if it had, would he wish to continue the association? On what terms?

Lauren sighed. She had no way of knowing. Mike would have to tell her what he expected. Then she could decide what to do.

She went into her small bathroom, resolved to be at her best for this very crucial evening.

The Carlos de Sevile showing.

And dinner with Mike in his suite afterward.

Chapter Five

Lauren had chosen to wear a dress of violet silk for the de Sevile showing. It had life, even under electric lights, yet it was subtle enough to play off Carlos's bold, dark colors and make a feminine statement. The silk was molded lovingly over Lauren's breasts and draped her slender waist, moving into a delightful triple row of horizontal gathers above her neatly rounded hips. From there it fell softly to the floor. It was simple, feminine, and provocative. Lauren hoped it would show de Sevile's heavy-handed designs for the unsuitable styles they were for most women in their thirties.

And this time, Lauren would be the one seated beside Mike. She wondered again what connection he had with the striking brunette who had been with him last night.

She brushed her golden hair until it shone, and did it up in a gleaming crown on her head. Adds a few inches, she thought, remembering the brunette's tall, svelte figure. Violet silk shoes and a silk shawl completed her ensemble. She picked up the small clutch purse, just large enough for her tiny lipstick, handkerchief, and the key to the suite.

A knock on the door startled her. She went quickly to open it, a smile on her lips. Instead of Mike, Herbert stood before her.

"I'm giving you one last chance, Lauren. Either agree to marry me or take the consequences."

"You know the answer to that, Herbert," she said quietly. "We were never friends. You were Al's friend. And we really don't even like each other. Can't we just let it drop?"

He glared at her. "So be it. You asked for whatever you get, lady." He turned and strode away.

Lauren closed the door, suddenly afraid. Herbert, like Al, prided himself on never forgetting or forgiving an injury. Often she had heard them recounting, with heavy laughter, the way one or the other of them had paid off a score against someone. But what had she done to Herbert? Only been angry at his efforts to sabotage her showing. Was that a crime? Determinedly she put thoughts of the unpleasant incident out of her mind. Herbert had no grievance against her. He would have a few drinks and forget all about her in the company of one of the younger women he favored.

She was making a final careful inspection of her person in the mirror when another knock sounded. This time she opened the door cautiously.

Mike waited outside, an exquisite, tiny purple orchid in his hand. He presented it with a bow. "I was sure your choice tonight would be your signature color. This matches your eyes." He bent to tie the velvet ribbon carefully around her wrist.

"You knew enough not to bring me something I'd have to pin on a shoulder." Lauren laughed, beaming with pleasure in the tiny, exquisite bloom.

"And thus ruin a costume over which you had spent hours?" He grinned. "Pin holes in that silk? Sacrilege."

"You are the perfect escort," Lauren told him, fluttering her lashes absurdly.

The wretch fluttered his right back at her. "And you,

my dear, the perfect escortee. Now we've got that off our chests, permit me to take you up to Carlos's tent-show. There'll be enough razzle-dazzle to satisfy everybody on board."

"Mike, you said you worked with Landrill's," Lauren ventured, as they strolled to the elevator. "Carlos is one of Landrill's designers. Shouldn't you be defending him?"

"Why? If he's good, he won't need defense. If he's not, he needs to be told!"

Lauren grinned. "Have you ever tried to tell our Spanish hidalgo anything? If so, how did you get him to listen?"

"Thank God I don't have to work with him," Mike said.

Lauren had to be satisfied with that, for there were other couples in the elevator, and no privacy. Mike led her to a seat near the front of the lounge, bordering on the runway.

"Aren't you afraid we'll get sideswiped by one of those eighty-pound skirts of the Sevillana collection?" teased Lauren, *sotto voce*.

"Meow!" her partner mocked. "Control your admiration, honey, or you'll have me thinking you're afraid of the guy!"

Lauren subsided, smiling. This man was something, she thought, glancing across at his big frame. He held himself well. He'd told her he was thirty-seven. It was a well-kept, trim, and vigorous body, nicely tanned but not playboy-teak; the face showing some laughter lines around the eyes and deep creases around the well-cut mouth, but no flab or fat. Lauren sighed. I hope he wants to mean something to me, she thought wistfully. Not just a shipboard romance.

With a wild flourish of toreador music, the de Sevile

presentation began. Glancing around as the lights lowered, Lauren decided it was the largest attendance she had seen so far; whatever else he had, Carlos had a good publicity campaign. Just as she was bringing her gaze back to the stage, Lauren caught a flash of diamonds against black lace. It was the woman Mike had squired last night, the statuesque brunette. She leaned unobtrusively nearer.

"There's a very beautiful brunette staring at you from the row just behind us," she whispered. "Should you speak to her?"

Mike turned casually, spotted the woman, and waved nonchalantly. Turning back, he grinned down at Lauren. "Jealous?"

"Should I be?" Lauren asked lightly.

"It all depends," the wretched man taunted. "Now watch the show, Mrs. Rose, honey. You might learn something from your competitor."

"Like what?" Lauren gritted.

"Like how *not* to design clothes," Mike said, obviously pleased with his own humor.

Lauren turned her attention to the runway, resolved to study the presentation with meticulous care. She knew she had much to learn, even from Carlos de Sevile, for he was a popular designer and famous among the "in" groups in the United States.

The show moved with slickly effective pacing: Burlington casuals, Wimbledon tennis outfits, luncheon at Buck House, tea at Harrods, afternoon formals for the Queen's Garden Party. . . .

"Carlos has gone British," Lauren gasped.

Mike grinned at her in the semiglow of the dimmed lights. "His wily tribute to Cunard," he murmured. "Carlos believes in grabbing on to a good thing."

Lauren was silent as the lavish, overstated presenta-

tion swayed and wiggled and flounced itself to a
conclusion, to the accompaniment of much heel-tapping
and some rather tasteless reprises of British popular
songs. The finale, called Royal Presentation, was intended to represent three debutantes being presented
at the palace, with their fond mama as presenter. The
mother looked, to Lauren's jaundiced eye, to be no
older than her daughters, and her gown was as laden
with flounces and feathers as theirs. One costume even
had a hoop to hold out the heavy skirt.

"I hope that thing's on wheels," Lauren muttered.
"The poor model will never be able to swing it on her
own."

"Naughty, naughty," Mike taunted. "Your professional jealousy is showing."

"I wouldn't be caught dead presenting those clothes,"
Lauren said, between her teeth. "You just wait until
you see my designs."

"I can hardly," Mike admitted with a grin. "We have
to stay here for a few minutes after the show," he
added, grinning. "To congratulate Carlos, you know."

"You stay," Lauren retorted. "I'll meet you for dinner later."

Mike stopped smiling. "That's a promise," he warned
her. "Why don't you grit your teeth and stay here with
me? You won't have to jump up and down, you know.
Just be a good girl and tell Carlos nicely how pretty his
dresses are."

Lauren knew he was teasing her, but she couldn't
find the situation amusing. Carlos had snubbed and
bad-mouthed her so arrogantly she wasn't hypocrite
enough to tell him she admired his heavily ornate
costumes.

"Half an hour, in your suite," she said, and got up to
leave.

She had to move against the stream, as many of the audience were crowding up to the runway to congratulate Carlos, who, resplendent in white tailcoat, was posing for pictures in a garland of his models. Lauren finally made her way out of the lounge, to be buttonholed by a young man she had seen the first evening at the cruise director's meeting to set up the program. He was one of the polished youths who had fluttered around Carlos when the designer came to see what September Song was doing.

"Rose?" the young man said, placing himself in her way.

"I am Lauren Rose, yes," she said quietly.

"Señor Carlos instructed me to warn you that nothing but a legitimate fashion show will be permitted."

Lauren raised her eyebrows. "Indeed? What is that supposed to mean?"

"There have been rumors," the youth explained loftily. "Word is out that you have some plan to put on a burlesque show tomorrow afternoon—"

"I'd never attempt to outburlesque the sideshow Carlos put on tonight," Lauren said sweetly. "So vulgar it was almost classic." She moved aside deftly. "Forgive me, will you? I need some Alka Seltzer."

The youth stamped his foot petulantly, but Lauren moved away with a laugh. Who had run to Carlos with that bit of gossip? Dani? Nella? Not likely, although Dani might have discussed it in someone's hearing. Herbert? Did he know? He had enough ill-will to invent such a story on even a hint of her plan. Did he have a hint? Surely not from Mike, who had said he despised Herbert. Shrugging, Lauren went down to her suite to freshen up before her dinner with Mike. She had hardly let herself into the sitting room when the phone rang. It was Tony, in a hurry.

"We've run into a snag," he explained. "Can we borrow the clothes we are to wear, so I can check the choreography and timing?"

"Yes, of course," Lauren answered. "I'm here for the next half-hour. Borrow a rack from the purser's office. I'll throw a sheet over it. Can you and Derek come right away?"

"See you," Tony said briskly.

Within five minutes there was a subdued knock on the door. Lauren let the two men in and began transferring the clothes to their rack. As she hung up the jewel of her collection, she begged, "Please bring them back the minute you've finished?"

Derek looked grave. "It may be long after midnight. Will you mind waiting up to let us in?"

Lauren considered. She might very likely be in Mike's suite at that hour. She couldn't risk having the men wake Dani or Nella. Reluctantly she made up her mind to a rather dangerous course of action.

"Keep the clothes overnight. Have you some safe place to lock them up? Don't leave them in the gym."

"Violet and I have a small cabin, but it's all ours." Derek grinned. "I'll sit up all night with a shotgun."

"Do that," Lauren smiled, watching Tony roll the sheet-covered rack to the outer door. "I appreciate all you're doing for me."

"Think nothing of it," Derek whispered, helping Tony out the door with the rack. "See you at eight sharp, luv."

Lauren washed her face, freshened her makeup, and took her hair down out of its coronet. She brushed it until it shone, and let it flow softly to her shoulders. Then she tied a narrow violet silk scarf around it to hold it off her face. Finally, she donned a dark-purple cape lined with mauve silk.

There could be no all-night meeting tonight. She had to be at the early rehearsal the next day, functioning well. Nothing must stand in the way of the agreement she had made with the Cunard Company to present the very best show of which she was capable. This was her priority: even love—if it *was* love between Mike and herself—must wait until she had kept her promise.

Pulling the cape more closely about her shoulders, she left the suite, locking the door carefully and securely behind her.

She walked up the stairs to Mike's suite, reluctant for some reason to use the elevators. As she approached his rooms, she could hear music and laughter. Was Mike entertaining others besides herself? Frowning, Lauren hesitated near the outer door of his suite. A laughing couple, coming up behind her, forced her to step aside. They rapped lightly on the door and went in, leaving it ajar. A babble of talk, laughter, shouts and music flooded the hallway. The sitting room was crowded. In a momentary gap caused by the movement of the crowd, Lauren caught a flash of Mike. He was standing with a champagne glass in his hand, talking to the statuesque brunette and Carlos de Sevile.

Lauren turned away and went back down the corridor. This time she took the elevator to her own deck. She had a fleeting wish to seek the dark serenity outside, but her heart was too sore.

She undressed quietly after locking the outside door, and tried to get to sleep. Eight o'clock would come soon enough and the models must be roused and fed by seven at the latest. This was much better, she decided. She had been foolish to think of spending several hours with Mike tonight, with her show set for the next day. Why had she even considered it?

Because you are a fool, she told herself harshly.

Thinking you had found the perfect mate, a man you could love with all your heart and mind and body, when in fact all you have found is a man who can't even remember he has invited you to dine in his suite. Of course, a man-of-the-world isn't looking for a romantic attachment. One-night stand is more his style, she lashed herself. Isn't it about time you acted your age, woman? A man with his virile charm doesn't have to settle for some thirty-five-year-old widow. He's more likely to marry the Dark Lady whose diamonds and costumes bespoke both taste and breeding. At which point she began to cry, soundlessly, bitterly, into her pillow.

And the telephone beside her bed rang.

She wouldn't have answered it, except that she was afraid the ringing would wake the models. She lifted the receiver.

"Yes?" she said in a small, husky voice.

"You're late," Mike said quietly in her ear.

"I'm surprised you missed me in that crush," Lauren heard herself saying.

There was a slight pause, and then he said, "I've got rid of them now, Lauren. Come to dinner. It's waiting to be served."

Lauren felt very contrary. "Why should I?"

"Because I'm hungry," Mike said, in a surprised voice.

Lauren couldn't help herself. She chuckled softly.

"That's better," he said smugly. "C'mon up."

"I'm in bed," she said ungraciously.

"Shall I come down?" he asked.

"I'll come," Lauren groaned softly. "There's no food here, and I'm hungry, too."

Mike hung up with a laugh, and Lauren got up and dressed again. This time she put on a dark purple suit with a mauve silk shirt. If she was going to come back after midnight, she told herself, she wasn't going to look like Cinderella. This was the suit she had intended wearing for the rehearsal, but she refused to let herself consider the implications of that. She did *not* intend to spend the night with Mike; it was just that she'd already laid out these clothes for the morning. They were handier.

Who am I kidding? she thought as she relocked the outside door and took the elevator up to Mike's deck. The door was closed this time and no sounds of revelry came from behind it. Lauren knocked softly. The door swung open. A steward was busy clearing away glasses and trays of hors d'oeuvres, napkins and ashtrays. Mike held his hand out with a warm smile.

"Welcome to the battlefield. Henry swears he'll have this mess cleaned up in five minutes, and have our dinner set up in five more." He drew her inside and closed the door as he spoke.

Henry was as good as his word. Within five minutes he had the sitting room clean and the terrace doors standing open to air away the fumes of cigars and cigarettes. He rolled the refuse out on his trolley. Mike took Lauren out onto the deck to watch the waves as they raced past.

"This is where I wanted to be," Lauren confessed. "I was . . . a little surprised to find out that you'd invited so many guests to dinner."

"In the first place, I didn't invite them," Mike said with a wry expression. "Knowing Carlos, you should be able to reconstruct that script. He just swept everyone along on the wave of his own bumptious self-interest. You know he works for Landrill's. I owed him a celebration after his 'triumph,' I believe was the way he put it. He even invited all the judges."

"Did they come?" Lauren was fascinated at such one-upmanship.

"Reb Crowell did. He loves the scent of a story. The others properly refused him, apparently. Carlos said something about uppercrust snobbery, which ill-suits his claims to be a member of the minor nobility himself. He's as vulgar as his designs."

"You'd think Landrill's would get rid of him," Lauren said waspishly.

"His contract doesn't run out until next year," Mike informed her.

"How did you get rid of them all?" Lauren was curious. The last time she'd seen this room, it was crowded with zealous merrymakers.

"I told them about the big party Landrill's had arranged to celebrate Carlos's showing. We've taken over the Players Club for the rest of the night, in case anyone wants to gamble; a buffet supper is being served in the Queen's Grill; dancing later on the Lido Deck. Carlos couldn't resist the splash—a de Sevile Night on the *QE II*. He'll probably spend the rest of it running from one place to another to collect applause. And how do *you* expect to spend the rest of the night?" He put the simple question to her with devastating unexpectedness.

The man was taking an unfair advantage, Lauren thought, by sneaking in that particular question. He was standing over her, so close that she could feel the heat emanating from his body and the strength of his virile attraction. She had never seen anything as sensual as his smile. It was a hard, wolfish grin, revealing his white teeth, those teeth that had closed so gently over her earlobes, her lower lip, her nipples . . .

Lauren closed her eyes. She didn't want to think of what had happened after he had roused her nipples to hard, rosy buttons. No man had ever before touched her that way, evoked in her that amazing, unexpected thrill that had pierced her whole body with a pleasure as sharp as pain.

Mike would not permit her to withdraw. He took her in his arms, pulled her close to his big, warm body. Lauren shivered.

He set her free at once. "Are you cold? We'll go back inside."

When they were once more in the softly lighted sitting room, Lauren expected Mike would take her in his arms again. Instead, he took a cigarette from a box and lit it, watching her, frowning.

"What is it?" she asked somewhat nervously.

"It's that damned suit. More like a coat of mail. Why did you change out of that sexy thing you had on for the show? I was looking forward to taking it off you, very slowly. And with appropriate ceremonies."

Lauren couldn't meet the wicked provocation in his face. Nor could she think of anything to say. Any bits of bright repartee she might have come up with to divert his intent assault on her senses had vanished. His keen gray eyes were too knowledgeable to be fobbed off with anything but the truth. Lauren, completely aware of every inch of his splendid body, was completely vulnerable to him. They both knew she would do anything he asked of her.

Henry entered then with the food trolley, saving her for the moment. Grinning at her obvious relief, Mike ushered her into her chair across from his at the round table. Henry had set it with crisp linen and heavy silver and a vase containing a single rose. Lauren noticed Mike's glance traveling from the flower to Henry's imperturbable face. It was evident that the steward's sense of occasion amused her host.

The meal was actually a rather silent one. The food

was superb, as it had been the night before. In fact, Lauren commented that she had never had a poor meal on the ship. Mike treated this diversionary remark with smiling silence. To her surprise, Lauren did full justice to each course, including the coffee and the dessert, a meringue cup filled with dark cherries and whipped cream.

Mike settled her on the big couch and handed her a liqueur. "To relax you." He grinned ominously. Henry said good night.

Lauren faced him at last—this big, smooth, inscrutable man who had become, in the space of four days, incredibly important in her life. And then she surprised herself.

"Who is the brunette with the diamonds?" she heard herself asking.

Mike seemed less surprised at the question than Lauren was. "Her name is Buffy Hardacre Landrill. She's the temporary sister-in-law of the owner."

"Temporary?"

"She's in the process of getting a divorce from Christopher Landrill. All very amicable and, of course, lucrative for the lady."

Lauren frowned. "I don't like the sound of that."

"My dear, the laborer is worthy of her hire," Mike said in a mocking tone that disturbed Lauren. She wished she had never brought up the subject. Still, she had, and now she must pursue it.

"I'm not interested in the marital affairs of the Landrills," she explained. "I meant your *tone* was so . . . cynical. All women are not just out for what they can get, you know. Some of us take pride in our own independence."

"Don't tell me you're a libber," Mike taunted. "One

look at you and a man knows how delightfully you
could cling."

"I am a responsible professional woman," Lauren
protested, angrier than she wanted to be. Clinging vine,
indeed. "You do know I am the designer for September Song line, don't you? A successful businesswoman?
And I didn't get there hanging on some man's coat
sleeve."

Mike laughed. "I'm not talking about your business
experience, which is more than admirable. I'm refer-
ring to your way with a man you take a fancy to."

"There's only been Al," Lauren told him. "I don't
sleep around." And then she was horrified to feel a hot
blush mount to her cheeks. Had she not just spent the
previous night sleeping in Mike's bed? She raised an-
guished eyes to meet his gaze. "I mean—"

"I know what you mean." The cynical note had gone
out of his voice and he smiled at her lazily. "And *that*
means that you must have felt something special about
us?"

Lauren nodded. "I've never felt this way before."

Mike sipped at his liqueur. He wasn't smiling now,
Lauren noticed. After a minute he said, "We need to
talk about this. First, I must tell you that seldom, if
ever, have I felt—" He paused, frowned, then said in a
very different voice, "What a pompous ass I sound.
Meeting your splendid honesty with such an absurdity!
I know damn well I've never felt this way before, even
when I was married. Especially when I was married,"
he concluded grimly.

Lauren stared at him, her heart in her eyes. He came
to sit down beside her, took the glass from her fingers,
kissed her hard yet sweetly on the lips, murmured,
"Tasty," and then took her hand.

"I'm going to tell you the story of my life," he began,

reaching for a lighter note. "Specifically, my married life. I was twenty-six, graduated from Harvard and postgrad USC, when I met Lilith. Lilith Delmar," he explained.

Lauren had heard—who had not?—of the beautiful starlet whose sexual prowess had quite outshone her acting ability. Seven husbands—had Mike indeed been one of them? Lauren cast her mind back, trying to remember their names.

Mike shook his head, well aware of her confusion. "I'll tell you. She was just seventeen at the time, and I was her first husband. Michael Landrill."

Lauren drew in a sharp breath. No wonder Mike had one of the best suites on the splendid liner. Entrepreneur and talent scout indeed! But not as visible as some other multimillionaires, it seemed. Lauren couldn't ever recall having seen a photo of him in a newspaper or magazine. But Mike was going on.

"The charming Lilith stayed married to me for a year. By that time I was more than happy to pay the five million dollars she demanded to let me divorce her. It took quite a while for the wounds to heal." He looked at Lauren. "That's when I decided never to get caught in that particular trap again. You might say, once married, twice shy."

"I can understand that," Lauren said quietly. It was odd how quietly one's dream house can shatter and fall.

"I'm not against marriage as a general thing, for the propagation and protection of children. But I'm not sure I've the patience or the zest to be a father, and I wouldn't hamper a child with an uncaring parent. I've had that experience also."

Lauren was thinking that one would never know, to look at this fine man, that he was carrying such deep and still-painful scars. Uncaring parents, a vicious wife—what else could have happened?

Mike told her. "My younger brother, Chris, met and married Buffy when he was still in college. She encouraged him to drop out so that she could enjoy the ski-and-sun-fun life. He was badly injured at Gstaad last year and that gave Buffy her way out. Her lawyers and mine are negotiating the settlement now. I'm keeping my mouth shut until we have her signature on the dotted line, for Chris's sake. None of us want her to have second thoughts and decide to stay married to him."

There was a small silence, not comfortable. Then Lauren said, "Your brother and you have had a nasty experience with marriage. I can understand your refusal ever to be trapped again. My marriage, I'm coming to see, was unsatisfying on many levels. Still, I believe in marriage as a good way of life." She tried to smile. "I guess I'm just a cockeyed optimist!"

Mike frowned. "No recriminations because I didn't tell you my whole name sooner? No tears that I made love to you last night without a permanent relationship in mind? You are an unusual woman, Lauren."

Although he said it gently enough, Lauren sensed the deep wariness, the unhealed hurt behind the words. She gave him her best smile. "I wanted to make love to you as much as you needed me," she said quietly. "It was the most perfect thing that's ever happened to me, and I have no regrets. I hadn't planned on a—a shipboard romance when I came on the *Queen*, but I wouldn't have it different. And now I think I'll go along, Mike. I've got a dress rehearsal at eight o'clock, and my show hits the runway at two o'clock sharp." She got to her feet. She was shakier than she'd expected. She covered her slight stagger with a chuckle. "Too much of that good liqueur. Thank you for a wonderful dinner. And good night."

Mike was beside her, towering over her, his forehead creased into a thunderous frown. "What do you mean, good night? You're staying here with me. I haven't had enough of you yet."

Lauren saw the anger, hurt, and suspicion he was covering with the arrogant demand. She wasn't a promiscuous woman. The very idea of a one-night stand was abhorrent to her. And yet this was Mike, of the big, warm hands that had gently dried her feet; Mike, who had held off his own satisfaction for a long time while he brought Lauren to a full and delicious consummation. This was the man she could talk to, laugh with, be comfortable with. Love.

Her smile was natural and tender this time. "Of course, I'm staying," she said softly.

Mike's body relaxed, but he still had the wary expression on his face. "Want any more to drink or eat?"

Lauren shook her head, patting her stomach ruefully. "It's lucky I'm not needed to model the clothes tomorrow. I'm sure I've gained five pounds since we left New York."

Mike grinned and caught her up in his arms, swinging her off her feet and against his chest. He grinned, then mimed a stagger. "Phew! Closer to fifty pounds, Mrs. Rose. We'll have to work some of that off right now."

Looking up into his glinting gray eyes, set in their fan-shaped laugh wrinkles, Lauren realized that she loved him. Even his would-be-lecherous jokes seemed funny to her. So he didn't want to take a chance on being hurt again. She could understand that, although she didn't think there was much similarity between herself and a greedy, shallow seventeen-year-old starlet.

But Mike had his brother's failed marriage, and apparently an unhappy childhood, fixed in his mind as the inevitable result of marriage. It *wasn't* inevitable, but Lauren could understand his bias. He'd been taught in a hard school. She looked up into his face and knew she would never deliberately hurt him.

When he put her down beside his bed, he sat on the side of it and drew her in between his thighs. For a moment he stared up into her face, a questioning look so plain that Lauren impulsively pulled his head gently against her body.

"I love you, Mike."

He became very still in her arms. Then he leaned back and stared at her face. This time there was a hard, cold doubt in his expression.

"Is this a pity trip, Lauren?" he asked sharply. "If so, I don't want any part of it."

"Pity? For whom?" Lauren scoffed lovingly. "You know better than that, Mr. Gorgeous Mike Landrill. You were *here* last night. It was Christmas and Thanksgiving and the Fourth of July rolled into one package."

A grin broke slowly over Mike's face. "You do know how to make a man feel good, Lauren Rose," he said softly. He stood up and led her back to the sitting room.

Lauren went reluctantly. She had brought herself to the point of accepting what he was able to offer her, and now it seemed as though he were having second thoughts.

"Is something wrong?" she asked nervously.

"We've got to talk," he said in that deep, abrasive voice that set her nerves to tingling. "I have a special feeling for you, Lauren, but I'm not sure what it is. I sure as hell know what I *don't* want: marriage with you or any other woman." He brooded for a moment over

the idea. "I might conceivably decide to get married
someday, just to have a son, but I can't imagine doing it
in this decade, and by that time you'd be too old for safe
child-bearing. Although you might have made a good
mother if you hadn't been a professional woman." He
scanned her face and body darkly.

Lauren felt as though she had received a blow in the
stomach. How casually he had just cast away a dream
of hers, as if it were already too late for her. He
couldn't know how cruelly his remark had hurt. For
years she had tried to coax Al to start a family. He had
always said kids were a nuisance, that neither of them
had time, especially with her work, to bring them up. He
always managed to have a crisis or a problem about the
work to turn aside her plea. She turned her head away.

He seated her at one corner of the couch and took a
chair across from her. After a long, probing glance, he
said, "All right, Lauren, tell me what you expect from
me."

Lauren's head came up proudly. "I don't expect
anything, Mike Landrill. I knew from the beginning
that this was just a shipboard romance, a fling for you."
It seemed that that rankled; she hoped her voice hadn't
given her away. She tried for a sophisticated smile as
she concluded, "I expect you to say, 'Thank you, Lauren-
baby, for a lovely—a lovely . . .'" To her horror, she
couldn't complete the flip little sentence.

Mike was staring hard at her. "You know neither of
us feels that way about what's happened. Tell me what
you really think about us, Lauren."

She had to pull herself together and answer honestly
as a woman.

"I think you'll have to make your own decision about
what you want from our—our coming together on this
ship and finding a mutual attraction. I can't impose my

standards on you." She was trying to think her position through and explain it to him. She was happy to see that he was listening carefully, his eyes intent on her. She went on, slowly, "I've been married, and only now am I beginning to realize how unsatisfactory it was. Now that I've found something so much better." She smiled at him warmly. "It seems to me that people go through the motions—courtship, engagement party, wedding with gifts and guests and a reception and a honeymoon—all as if it's a sort of tribal custom. And somewhere there, the way the two people feel about each other gets lost. They've signed a life contract without reading the fine print, without considering the real reasons why a man and a woman would want to commit themselves. Sexual attraction, yes. We know how potent that can be." She gave him a slow sensuous smile that left him grinning. "But it's got to be more than sex. What would motivate a person to commit himself *for life* to some other person?"

"Now you're stating my point of view," Mike said. "People grow and change. Nothing remains the same. Why make promises you know you can't keep?"

Lauren nodded briefly. "I seem to have talked myself out of what my friends call 'a relationship.' "

Mike shook his head. "No, you've talked yourself out of the naïve romanticism of marry-and-live-happily-ever-after." He got up and came to sit beside her. He took her hand and turned her to face him. "But you haven't told me how you feel about some sort of a—a partnership with me. What do you see for us, Lauren?"

"I guess I haven't finished stating my position," Lauren said. She looked at him, and a bitter smile tugged at her lips. "One thing I never thought I'd do was enter into an academic discussion of the kind of affair I'd be willing to engage in. And yet I'm glad we had this talk,

Mike. Because I've discovered that, much as I believe
I've fallen in love with you"—she twisted her soft lips
cynically over the phrase—"I'm not ready to have a
brief sexual fling or even a longer-term liaison with
you. I'm being as honest as I can, Mike," she said as he
became hard-faced. "I'll wait for another idiotic romantic like myself, I think. A man who can visualize living
with me, sharing the hard going, reveling in the good
times, facing the challenges that might break up two
less caring people. Making it *work*, Mike. It's not easy
but I know one thing. And it's thanks to you that I finally
understand it."

"And what's that?" His voice was harsh, angry.

"That you have to care more about the other person's
pain than about your own. Isn't it crazy?" she asked.
"That old chestnut—'it hurts me more than it does you'—
it's true, Mike. I think that's what love means to me: that
I would rather be hurt than let my loved one suffer."
She got up at his shuttered expression with rueful eyes.
"I've sounded like a prig or a schoolgirl, I know. But
that's the way it is for me. I guess I've got to have a
man who wants me in the same way I want him."

"With a marriage license in one hand and a ring on the
other," Mike said bitterly. "I thought we had something
less commercial than that going for us."

Lauren frowned. "You've missed my point. It's not
commercial—it's sacred, a dedication. The ring is a vow,
not a payment. I'm sorry you can't see that."

Mike could see just how much she meant her words
by the look of pain and regret on her face. He said
shrewdly, "If you love me with the sort of love you claim,
and don't want to see me suffer, then you'll stay with me
tonight. Because if you don't, I'm going to suffer in more
ways than one." He took her slowly into his arms and
bent his head to take her lips with his mouth, at first

ently, and then, as he felt her response, with increasing arrogance, moving one hand inside her jacket to grasp her breast.

Conquered as much by love as by his use of her own argument, Lauren allowed herself to enter into the kiss fullheartedly. She did love Mike, whatever that meant to either of them. She wanted to satisfy his body, comfort his ego, make him feel strong and desirable and wanted. She gave herself ardently to the kiss, putting her arms around his shoulders and stroking as much of him as she could reach. She melded herself against his hardness, pressed her breasts and hips against him, softened her lips and opened them to his demanding mouth. She could feel his excitement burning hotter as her surrender roused him.

"Do you want me, Lauren?" he demanded, raising his dark head.

"I love you," she said softly. She wouldn't compromise.

The man stared into her face, reading the clear dedication there. Slowly he let her go, turned, and walked over to the door leading to the terrace. "It's gone flat, hasn't it? We've talked away the lovely lust we felt for each other. Was last night just a lucky fluke?" He was refusing to look at her, failing to see the steady light in her eyes. He shrugged. "Well, perhaps it was too much to expect, that anything that good could be repeated. I'll see you to your cabin."

"No, thank you." Lauren couldn't believe how calm her quiet voice was sounding, while, inside, something was tearing with a pain so hard it made her dizzy. "I'd rather go alone."

She heard his door close before she was three steps along the corridor. He wasn't going to come after her, pull her into his arms, tell her that it was all a mistake, that he loved her . . .

It was over.

Chapter Six

Ten minutes later, Lauren was sorry she had refused Mike's offer. She unlocked the door to the sitting room, relocked it from the inside, noted that the door to the models' room was closed, and slipped quietly into her own bedroom.

She was immediately aware of a heavy reek of wine. Oh, no, she groaned, not Herbert again. Switching on the light, she glanced quickly at the bed, fearful of seeing a red-faced, drunken man asleep on it. The bed was empty.

Lauren scanned the room. Her glance rested on the covered rack containing the new collection. She went to it at once to check on its safety. At least no one had taken it. But then she noticed that, near it, the stench of wine was stronger

Frantically, Lauren unzipped the cover. Then she stood, frozen, staring. One hand crept up to press against her lips. She blinked rapidly to clear her vision, unable, unwilling to believe . . .

Every garment on the rack had been liberally soaked with wine. Dark red and odorous, the heavy liquid still dripped from many of the costumes. The shoulders and tops of her new dresses and suits had the most massive stains . . . not removable even if she had time. It was wrecked. The whole new collection was ruined.

Although she knew it was no use, Lauren gently separated the dripping garments and tried to assess the damage. Was there anything usable left? The showing! Could she pull together a few outfits, enough to make some kind of presentation?

No. Whoever had done this had separated each hanger and doused its burden liberally. How many gallons does it take to ruin a collection? Lauren heard herself asking wildly.

She walked back and sat on the side of her bed almost mindlessly. She was finished. Aside from the destruction of months of work, there would be her public failure to present a fashion show tomorrow. How could she explain that to the Cunard officials who had given her this wonderful chance? Of course she could tell them about the ruined garments, but that wouldn't fill the runway for the final presentation of their special event. The event for which this very cruise had been set up. They would naturally wish to know what kind of security she had set up and how it had been breached.

Who would be this eager to see Lauren Rose fail? Carlos? How could he have gotten into her bedroom? The staff and crew of the *Queen Elizabeth II* were not people who could be bribed to open doors.

Herbert had had a key! On Sunday night he had been sprawled on the couch when she entered the sitting room. She tried to remember whether he had had a key or imposed on Dani. If he had a key, had he dropped it on a table before he left?

Lauren rubbed her forehead frantically. She must *think*. What was to be done? Go at once to the cruise director and tell her of the disaster, of course. And then find Derek and tell him—

Derek! Her eyes widened with incredulous joy. He

and Tony had wheeled out a whole rack of the costumes, everything they would be wearing for their presentation, before she had left for Mike's suite. September Song still had a show! Incomplete, yes—quite failing to do justice to her planning and the seamstresses' inspired sewing—but a show. Lauren dropped to her bed and lay there, a hand over her eyes, too busy planning to cry.

She waited until after breakfast to tell Nella and Dani about the vicious sabotage. With the air-conditioner going all night, she had cleared out some of the reek from her bedroom, but a steward would have to be summoned to remove the sodden mess and clean up the carpet. She ordered breakfast to be served in the suite, preferring to keep the models as unflustered as possible, and well away from prying eyes that might note their reactions. While she was waiting, she dressed in the suit she had worn to Mike's cabin the night before, let her hair fall in its natural soft waves to her shoulders—she didn't think she could endure a single pin or clasp—and then went to rouse Nella and Dani.

Dani at once noticed the faint redolence of wine. "Had a little party last night, Ms. Rose?" she gibed.

Lauren went to the door of her bedroom, opened it, and pointed. Both girls crowded forward to look, gasped, and turned stricken faces toward her.

"Who did it?" Nella gasped.

"Someone who got a key from somewhere, or who was let in," Lauren said slowly. "Did either of you let anyone in last night?"

"I left the door open for the doctor," Nella wailed. "It's all my fault." She gulped. "But I don't see why *he* would want to ruin our show," she added wretchedly.

"I'm sure he didn't," Lauren told her. "But an open

door was an invitation to anyone to enter." She squared her shoulders. "Not to worry—as our English friends say. I think I can handle it."

"What are we going to do?" demanded Dani.

Lauren felt a wave of gratitude at that partisan "we".

"We've still got all the clothes the troupe are going to wear for their act. Thank God, they needed them last night to iron out some problem in their presentation. That means there's enough costumes for us to do some sort of modified showing. The great dress is safe." That was the way they had referred to the jewel of Lauren's collection, the velvet, sequin, and chiffon creation that Lauren believed was the most beautiful gown she had ever designed. It was certainly the most original.

"Will you make an announcement about the sabotage?" Dani asked.

"I haven't gotten that far," Lauren admitted. "I've been awake half the night thinking what sort of presentation I can make with two-thirds of the clothes gone. We've got shoes and accessories, but what they'll fit in with, I'm still trying to work out."

Nella said surprisingly, "I think it was that Mr. Masen. He hates you, Ms. Rose."

Lauren and Dani stared at the tall woman in surprise.

"You could be right," Dani said. "Look at how the rat has acted. Can you pin it on him, Lauren?"

It was the first time Dani had ever called her anything but "Ms. Rose" and Lauren felt supported by the friendship. She said honestly, "I'm not sure I could prove it, and the hassle of making charges like that against a rat like Herbert might spoil our image. Let's just go into the show looking like brave little soldiers who are facing the challenge as best they can, eh? That ought to win us some support."

The models nodded dubiously. The saboteur's action

had been a shrewd blow against them as well as against Lauren, and they were angry and resentful.

They ate a good breakfast, which relieved Lauren of one of her fears. The models had taken it well, with a spirited resolve to beat the underhanded attacker at his rotten game. As soon as they had finished, Lauren shepherded them to the rehearsal room and briefly explained the problem to the troupe. They didn't say much, although the little they did say was too colorful to repeat. At least Lauren had a wonderful sense that their loyalty and total support were hers.

As she was leaving to consult with the steward about the removal and boxing up of the clothes—they might conceivably be needed as evidence—Nella said hesitantly, "Remember your color sketches of all the new collection, Lauren?" She looked embarrassed as they stared at her. "You know, you told us you were carrying a portfolio, in case any client asked to see some of the designs with a view to buying . . ."

"Yes, I've got the portfolio in my briefcase. When I found out we'd drawn last place in the program lineup, I didn't think I'd have time to discuss it with any prospective buyers. Why do you ask?"

"I thought we might put the sketches up on easels or something, and that would show everybody just what that rat Masen spoiled."

Lauren considered quickly. "I'll get them, unless—" Oh, God, Herbert knew about the sketches. Had he got at *them* too? She went on calmly, not wishing to disturb her team any more than they already were, "I'll check them while I'm in the cabin. Go on with your rehearsal, gang. I'll be back in a flash with snacks."

They've forgotten me already, Lauren thought as she heard the faint beat of music behind the locked door. It was good to see their dedication to her show. Lauren knew that even if everything didn't turn out, at least she'd made some real friends who meant more than any lounge full of wealthy patrons. Then she caught herself up. What kind of naïve idiot was she? You're a businesswoman, Rose, she told herself. Now you'd better prove it, for everyone's sake.

The steward, when he came, was properly horrified at the mess some vandal had made of Madame's clothing. He said it must be reported to the purser, and possibly even to the captain. Lauren explained about her showing that afternoon, barely five hours away. The man's concern was comforting, and, after telling her he would ask the purser to send someone down to her rooms at once, he left, pushing the ruined collection before him.

Lauren waited for the officer in the sitting room. When he came, Maida Hass was with him, and Reb Crowell. Maida, her expression concerned and helpful, asked the expected questions.

"I can't be sure who did it," Lauren confessed. "I was out of the cabin until almost midnight and the models were asleep in their own cabin. Whoever did it worked quietly."

"And had a key or access," added the reporter.

"That idea worries me," the cruise director confessed. "The Line—"

"I can reassure you," Lauren said quickly. "I am convinced no member of the staff would supply entrance to any unauthorized person." She hesitated. "There is a good chance that my husband's friend, Mr. Herbert Masen, got a key from one of the models the first day out. She wouldn't have suspected anything, since he is, actually, a shareholder in my business, September Song."

"Do you intend bringing charges, Mrs. Rose?" asked the officer quietly.

Lauren shook her head. "No. At this point, that sort of fuss would detract from my presentation and cause an unpleasant situation without solving anything."

"You intend going on with the show?" Reb asked incredulously. "I thought your costumes were ruined."

Lauren looked around at the three people in her cabin. Every face was friendly, interested. "May I trust you not to say anything about all this until after the show today?"

They nodded, and the reporter grinned. "I told you I'd mention your name, Mrs. Rose, and I sure will, but not until you've made your comeback. Just how do you plan to put on a show with no costumes?"

Lauren smiled. "That's the break I got. Not all the costumes were on the rack. About one third of them were in a small room we requested for secret rehearsals. You see I got an idea . ." And she told them about the dance troupe and the special presentation. "By the most wonderful stroke of luck, Mr. Derek Strange needed the costumes I'd assigned for their performance, and he and Tony called for them last night. They're safe. Right now the troupe is working on details with my models and we're going to put on a show."

Lauren was surprised and almost in tears when the three people clapped heartily.

Maida said firmly, "I think you're right about not making trouble before the show, but I do think an announcement could be made just before we start this afternoon. Think of the suspense! I'll handle that part."

The officer smiled and shook her hand. "You're showing splendid spirit, Mrs. Rose, if I may be permitted to say so. Courage and restraint." He shook his head. "My own impulse would be to knock the fellow sideways." Lauren laughed and mimed a punch.

Reb grinned at her. "Feisty, aren't you? What a story

this is going to make. Don't worry, I'll hold it until after the show. In the meantime, if it's not illegal or unethical, I'd like to wish you the best of luck, Lauren." He too shook her hand.

When they had left, Lauren wasted no time returning to the room where the rehearsal was going on. She ordered sandwiches and beer and coffee to be sent in, and stood guard by the door to take in the trolley herself when it arrived.

The rehearsal was going well. It seemed that the sabotage had brought the determination and creative skill of the dancers to a high point. Even Nella and Dani were being helpful, offering sensible and practical advice, demonstrating the model's walk and postures so Tony could mime them. He did so with such gusto and wit that even Nella was soon chuckling and Dani didn't seem offended at his sly little jokes about her profession. Lauren, dispensing food and drink, could hardly believe the feeling of comradeship they were all sharing. And gradually a presentation was emerging that combined the best of a formal fashion showing with some delightful comedy and graceful, costume-flattering dances. Lauren wondered if she dared breathe a sigh of relief yet, and then superstitiously crossed her fingers.

During the few minutes when Derek was not rehearsing, Lauren told him about the colored sketches of her whole new collection, safe in her briefcase. He was very interested and advised her to put them on display.

"It's proof, if any is needed, that you did have a terrific collection. And the sketches will show what it looked like. I'd be willing to wager you might even get some takers—or buyers, or clients, or whatever you high-fashion types call it." He stared at her thoughtfully for a moment. "What we need here is visibility.

Taping them on the walls of the lounge wouldn't do. So where?"

Lauren tried to think of something original and couldn't. She hadn't enough assistants to have them parade with the large, colorful sketches.

Derek gave a sound of triumph. "Got it, I think. What are the runways made of?"

"Wood, usually."

"How high are they—off the ground, I mean? About four feet?"

"Something like that," guessed Lauren, who'd never thought about it before.

"Then we'll tape the designs on the sides of the runway, so everyone can see them and can't tear or deface them without all the rest of the people in the row witnessing the act. Tell Maida Hass before the show. I know they close the lounge for an hour before a presentation to be sure everything's clean and shipshape."

"You do have a fund of knowledge," Lauren teased, delighted at his suggestion. "I'll take the sketches to Maida right away. That is, if you think you can spare me from this rehearsal?" She chuckled.

"We'll manage," Derek said.

Maida was more than willing to help in any way possible. She promised to have the sketches taped up around the runway. "If I can tear myself away from them long enough to have it done," she admitted, drooling over the brilliant, colorful drawings.

Lauren returned to her cabin, feeling breathless and frightened and full of gratitude all at the same time. Her phone was ringing as she unlocked the door. She swung it closed behind her and ran to catch the call.

It was Mike Landrill.

"I need to see you, Lauren."

"My showing is in a couple of hours, Mike. May I see

you afterward?" Lauren was surprised that she had breath to answer him, so fiercely was her heart pounding in her breast.

There was a little pause. "What's wrong?" Mike asked softly.

"You mean you haven't heard? Ship security must be tighter than I suspected, or else Herbert's ashamed to boast that he ruined my collection," Lauren said. She hadn't intended to tell anyone. She wasn't even aware that the words were there until she heard them herself.

And then she heard him say, in that deep dark voice that so excited her, "Stay there. I'll be right down."

Is that what I wanted? she asked herself. Then she ran into her cabin and checked her makeup and brushed her hair until it gleamed and shone like white gold.

She hardly had time to return to the sitting room before there was an imperative knock on the door and Mike entered. His nostrils flared at the pervasive smell of wine.

"What happened?"

Lauren told him. His face became stone-hard. "What have you done about it?"

"The cruise director knows. So do the judges, by now—Reb Crowell was here. I've asked them all to say nothing until after the showing this—"

"Showing?" Mike interrupted. "What will you show?"

Lauren explained about the clothes the troupe had taken away.

"So some of your lovely designs were saved," Mike said slowly. "And, being you, of course you're going ahead with what's left. Well, I congratulate you. And no, I won't talk about it, or break Masen's neck as I should do. Was Carlos de Sevile in on it?"

Lauren shrugged. "I don't know. I haven't even seen Herbert today, much less accused him. And I may not ever do that. I'm just tired of the whole chintzy mess. The dancers and my models have been so good, so supportive. I feel blessed just knowing how fine some people are."

Mike looked at her intently. "No raging desire for blood? No revengeful counterplans? I'm getting to know you under fire, Lauren. What's that academic handle— Professor Emeritus? You know it means a title won in the heat of battle? I'm going to call you Lauren, Designer Emeritus."

He smiled for the first time since he'd entered the cabin. Then he came to her and took her in his arms. It was so natural, so sweet, so *right*, that Lauren forgot her resolutions and relaxed against him in perfect peace. After a moment, he rocked her gently, a slight motion, but one that made her very conscious, for the first time, of his hard body against her softness. She caught in a deep breath of the lovely male smell of him, clean flesh, a spicy cologne, fresh linen.

"You smell good," she whispered.

His body telegraphed laughter to hers, and he drawled, "I think you do too, but it's hard to tell with so much wine in the air. Come up to my stateroom and we'll investigate."

Lauren, drugged with the unexpected pleasure of being held in his arms again, was ready to agree to anything when the phone rang.

"Never a dull moment," she murmured, reluctantly releasing herself from his possessive hold.

He followed her to the telephone and, standing close behind her, took her breasts in his hands. Lauren almost hung up, so keen was the excitement that firm grip roused in her.

"Hello?" she managed.

The next instant she was upright and holding the

receiver to her ear tightly. "Why, hello, Lady Winston-Bell," she stammered.

"I've just heard of the dreadful thing that happened to your collection, Mrs. Rose, and your very gallant intention to present the dresses you have left. I wonder if you have time to see me for just a few minutes? I know how frantically busy this morning must be for you, and I can come to your cabin at once if that is convenient?"

"Of course, I shall be delighted," said Lauren.

When she hung up, she told Mike what was hapening. "I suppose she wants to reassure you, or something," he murmured discontentedly. "*I* wanted to comfort you."

He was so much like a small boy denied a treat that Lauren grinned. Then, greatly daring, she said, "Perhaps you'd like to invite me to dinner in your suite again?" Third-time lucky, her heart prompted.

"I'm taking you to the Captain's Dinner tonight," Mike said casually. "I want to be there when we hear who won."

"I'd love to go with you to the dinner," Lauren said. To have him near her, beside her—whether the evening produced pain or triumph—that would be security. The kind of thing a married couple would do, she told herself, but didn't say so to Mike.

He left, and Lauren hastily checked the cabin and opened the window to assist in dispersing the still-lingering wine odor.

When Lady Winston-Bell arrived, Lauren led her to a chair and sat down across from her. The older woman took no time for idle chatter. "I understand your models were working with some of your costumes when this terrible thing happened. Did you save enough to put on a show?"

"Yes, with the kind of performance I have envisioned," Lauren said quietly. "I know you don't want to hear the details, since you will be judging our presentation this afternoon. Maida Hass intends to announce the sabotage, but I do wish to give a modified showing."

"I am so pleased you are taking the dastardly blow so gamely." She smiled at Lauren. "I must tell you that I have requested a brief meeting with each designer, so that I may understand the theory, the artistic intention, behind the style of each collection. Would you tell me what you feel is the particular motivation behind your designs?"

"Yes, I'd like that," Lauren answered cheerfully. "I like to believe that a woman does not need to become either a vegetable or a wax dummy on the eve of her thirtieth birthday. She is still the same warm, vital, creative human being she was the day before. If she has taken intelligent care of her body and stimulated her mind, she should be able to function in every way as a woman until she is twice that age."

Lady Winston-Bell laughed delightedly. "You only give us sixty years, Mrs. Rose? Conservative of you!"

Lauren returned her guest's pleasant smile. "I was once told that the whole body regenerates or rebuilds itself every seven years. And recently I read that there is a perfect pattern for reconstruction in every cell. Why shouldn't these patterns continue to create good cells for us?" She chuckled at the look on the other woman's face. "No, I'm not trying to start a cult; I'm just optimistic, life-oriented, busy, happy. And I seem to be making it work, somehow. But, as for growth, I believe it brings change also. The clothes that suited me when I was five or fifteen or twenty-five are not suitable for me today."

"In other words, you think a woman doesn't get older, she just gets better?"

"Something like that. Didn't Shakespeare say, 'ripeness is all'? Aren't the greatest vintages *mature* ones? Life gives us time to learn to appreciate the rarest wines, time to build relationships that are strong and able to weather the storms." Lauren caught herself up. "Do forgive me, Lady Winston-Bell. I am giving a lecture rather than answering simply."

The older woman rose gracefully to her feet, her smile warm and reassuring. "You've told me exactly what I wished to hear: your philosophy of design. No wonder your own clothes are so beautifully simple and suitable. And so pretty."

Lauren thanked her and saw her to the door. Then she sank down into a chair and wondered what other surprises this day would bring. She immediately jumped up, shocked that she could, even momentarily, have forgotten that September Song would be presenting an unusual fashion show within two hours. She hurried to don the simple, elegant violet silk dress she had chosen for the occasion.

The next two hours were hectic, but the enthusiasm of her team carried them and Lauren toward the moment of truth. Ten minutes before the Royal Court Lounge was opened to the public, Lauren knew they had done all that eight human beings could do. Even the small orchestra, having heard of the destruction of most of Mrs. Rose's costumes, seemed determined to support her with their most careful and spirited playing. Maida was quietly helpful, making sure that coffee and broth were available, checking the stage and the curtains she had had installed across the arch.

Lauren stood at a lookout behind one of the side screens. At this moment, it seemed to her that for all their efforts her team was doomed to fail, not through any fault of their own, but because there would be no audience to evaluate the designs. The judges were already in place, their small table and scoring sheets before them. Besides the three of them, so few people sat in the comfortable chairs that Lauren's heart sank. Had someone spread the word among the first class passengers that the show wasn't worth bothering about? Was it known that her costumes had been ruined? Lauren resolved that her show would go on if only these few people watched it.

And then Herbert strolled in, with his youthful girlfriend clinging to his arm. Lauren saw him glance around as he sat down near the runway—in a position to gloat, thought Lauren—counting the poor attendance with satisfaction. Just you wait, Herbert Masen, just you wait.

There was a stir at the entrance. People began to stream into the room—well-dressed, laughing people. Soon the seats were comfortably filled, and still new arrivals entered and searched for places. Lauren could hardly believe her eyes. And then she saw Mike, big and darkly handsome in a lounge suit that had surely been made in London. Mike Landrill was shepherding the influx of guests, smiling broadly. Lauren couldn't believe the warmth of the feeling of gratitude that rose within her. Mike was acting like a partner. No, more than a partner. She turned to the troupe and caught Derek's eye. There was determination in her own.

"Ready?" she called to him.

He nodded, grinning.

Lauren gestured to the leader of the musicians. The strains of "A Pretty Girl Is like a Melody" drifted gently through the lounge. The curtains drew slowly back, revealing a boutique at night. Two artificial mannequins on platforms were revealed, dressed in costumes that gleamed and glowed softly in the dim light. The mannequins posed rigidly, their makeup indicating that they were lay figures. Slowly the lights brightened. A baby spot focused on one figure. It was Nella. Her red hair glowed in the light. She was wearing a sheath of bronze silk that clung lovingly to her splendid figure and enriched the luster of her hair. As with most of the September Song dresses, this one had no busy details or ornaments to distract the eye from the pure, flowing line of the design and the body in it. While the murmur of pleasure was still rising from the audience, a second spotlight came on, revealing Dani in the jewel of Lauren's collection.

Dani looks like a princess, Lauren thought. The way most of us dream of looking. Her head of glistening black curls was held proudly. The small body wore the lovely dress with such verve that, even frozen into position, the gown shimmered. There were audible gasps of appreciation as the musicians paused for a moment before moving triumphantly into "Love Is a Many-Splendored Thing".

The ivory velvet of the bodice was artfully sewn with pastel sequins, gentle yet erotic. From the waist, soft floats of chiffon in pastel colors flowed to Dani's ankles, and though they were, of course, motionless now, Lauren knew how they would sway and shift enchantingly as the wearer walked or danced, revealing a brief tantalizing glimpse of thigh or ankle. The costume was a celebration of femininity. The audience loved it, applauding generously.

A tiny chill went over Lauren's skin. Those were her two best designs. She had given her strongest cards away, and the show was just beginning. Normally the greatest design was saved to crown and climax the

showing. Then she shrugged and forced herself to
relax. Nothing in this performance was normal, routine.
She had better keep her mind on the job of helping the
performers into and out of their costumes.

A change in the music announced the entrance of
the cleaning women. The lighthearted, irreverent "With
a Little Bit of Luck" caused laughter as Violet, Polly,
and Dolly strolled in, impudently examined the gowns
of the rigid mannequins. Although she was seeing it
from the back, Lauren had to chuckle at the hilarious
mime Tony had created for the women. Their heads
were swathed in cloth, to protect the elaborate coiffures
they would need to display after they donned the beautiful gowns from the collection. Their work clothes
were gray, kimonolike garments that effectively dis-
guised the essential undergarments. They mimed around
the mannequins, peacocking absurdly with their brooms
and dusters, until one of them, Violet, made a decision.
Calling the other two close, she mimed a proposal to
which the others heartily agreed. Then, very carefully,
they pulled the stand bearing Dani back behind the
screens.

At once Lauren was ready to assist Dani out of the
costume and put Polly in it. While this was happening,
Dolly and Violet pulled Nella's platform behind the
screen as Polly prepared to go on stage.

Tongue in cheek, the musicians played "Here She
Comes, Miss America" as Polly danced on stage. Then,
followed by a pink spot, Polly danced down the runway,
apparently in a dream of joy. This was well received;
the applause was generous.

By the time Polly had returned to the stage, Violet
was out, dressed in the bronze silk, which flattered her
newly bronzed hair. Her movements, at first awkward,
to carry out the idea of the cleaning woman's inexpert-

ness as a model, gradually changed as the music swelled into "Where Is Love?" And then Derek and Tony entered, in black leotards and tights with large security-guard patches on their shoulders. Polly and Dolly came running in, dressed in delicate afternoon gowns. There was a mimed chase as the guards attempted to catch the women. For this amusing scene, the orchestra played an hilarious mélange of classical czardas, a pizzicato from "Sylvia," which cried out for the tiptoeing chore-ography Tony had chosen, and then an absurd segue into "Camptown Races". The audience, tickled with the mood music, enjoyed the dancing tremendously.

Then the tempo changed. The guards caught the cleaning women and held them, but instead of an offi-cial grip, the contact became a slow dance of invitation and acceptance. For this, the orchestra played Viennese waltzes. The men slipped away behind the screens and changed into formal evening wear, reentered the stage, and bowing, requested the pleasure of the dance. Violet, in the bronze silk, was the first led out, by Derek. The two tall dancers swayed and swung to the music as though in a dream. The man's head was bent adoringly over the woman's. They smiled. The women in the audience loved it.

Then, as Derek returned his partner to the stage, Tony moved down the runway with Dolly. Derek fol-lowed with Polly in the jewel dress. Their sensuously rhythmic movements displayed Lauren's designs per-fectly. Tony had choreographed this part of the dance to emphasize the beauty-in-motion of the long chiffon "leaves". Again, the audience received the effort with enthusiastic applause.

And then, to the dismay of most of the audience, the lights began to dim. At first the dancers did not notice; then, as the music took on a gentler note, they seemed to become aware that the party was over. To the rather mournful notes of "Good Night, Sweetheart", the guards returned the cleaning women to the stage and brought back the platforms. By this time Nella was again robed in her bronze dress and the men carried her out and placed her on her platform. A musician sounded twelve strokes of midnight on his chimes. The pensive mood was most delightfully and unexpectedly broken by the hasty entrance of the guards bearing Dani—in her exquisite bridal underwear! As they set her on her platform, the baby-pink spot lighted her delicious contours, to the guards' obvious consternation. Tony rushed backstage, caught the evening cloak Lauren was holding ready, ran back on, and flung the cape about the pretty figure just as the last note struck. The audience loved this little scene, especially the men.

Then the lights went out and the curtains were drawn across the stage.

Lauren had been concentrating so hard on helping with costume changes that she had scarcely had time to listen to the audience's reaction to the show. She did hear—after the first few startled moments when the audience was apparently shocked into silence by the unusual nature of the show—scattered applause, laughter, and the silence that denotes absorbed attention. When the final curtain came, there was a minute of absolute silence. Lauren clenched her hands so tightly that the nails cut into her palms. And then there was a crash, a barrage of clapping, and cries of "Bravo" and "Well done!" Lauren slumped against the wall, trembling. It was over and most of the audience evidently liked it.

Now she heard the well-bred, clear accents of Lady Winston-Bell. "What you have seen today, ladies and gentlemen, was the very courageous and successful attempt of a woman designer to give you a showing after two-thirds of her beautiful new collection had been deliberately ruined. By whom, it has not yet been determined, but investigations are being made."

There was a buzz of comment and exclamation from the audience. This was far more exciting than the average fashion show. Quite like the movies, in fact. Artistic sabotage, spies, secret forays by night!

Lady Winston-Bell resumed. "If you care to inspect the drawings that have been put up around the runway, you will see some of the lovely costumes Lauren Rose had hoped to please you with today. And now, a special tribute to a gallant lady, if you please." And she led another round of applause.

The curtains swung back and Derek and Tony, in the evening dress of their dance scene, led Lauren out onto the stage, and presented her to the audience. The applause became louder. Lauren smiled, bowed, and then curtsied to the judges, spreading the full violet silk of her skirt into softly rippling wings. When she turned to leave the stage, Derek and Tony again made themselves her escorts. The curtain closed. Backstage, the team fell into one another's arms, babbling with happiness and triumph.

"I think you might have a chance of winning," Dani said slowly. "I really didn't think so, until now. I just knew I had to help you, no matter how poor the show was. But it was great!" She looked at Tony soulfully. "Could you teach me some of those steps?" she asked, fluttering her long artificial eyelashes at him.

Back to her old tricks, thought Lauren. But she didn't have the heart to hold such tricks against a loyal member of the team, not when they'd pulled a show from the very depths of disaster.

In the next few minutes, however, it began to appear that they had not. A flurry at the entrance, voices rising above the cheerful chattering of the crowd, and then, when people were turning to see what the excitement was about, Carlos de Sevile came pushing through the departing audience like a small bright tugboat breasting heavy seas. At his shoulder, two of his assistants followed grimly. Carlos came to stand before the three judges, who were quietly talking near the runway.

"I demand to be heard," announced Carlos, very much aware of the numbers of guests who were watching him.

"What's with you, Señor Carlos?" Rebel Crowell asked. "Some of *your* designs sabotaged?" His glance was frankly skeptical.

"My collection was properly protected. Not left unguarded while the designer spent her time in—"

"I think you had something to tell us, Mr. de Sevile?" interrupted Lady Winston-Bell in a voice whose cool authority could not be denied. "Do so, please, without irrelevant comments."

Carlos glared at her, but his brash arrogance weakened before her calm, authoritative manner. "I wish to register a complaint," he blustered. "Ms. Rose has broken the rules of this Fashion Cruise by putting on a theatrical performance instead of a legitimate fashion show."

"Did you personally watch the alleged theatrical performance?" Reb gibed. "I seem to recall hearing that you were buying drinks last night and trying to dissuade people from attending."

Lady Winston-Bell frowned at the designer. "Are you making a formal charge without having seen the performance?" she asked.

Carlos shrugged. "I sent one of my assistants. He has just brought me the information."

"Then perhaps he should make the charge, since he

has the information and you don't," suggested Reb, who was obviously enjoying baiting the pompous designer.

"Mr. Crowell," Mrs. Cornelius warned, "this is not a joking matter. Serious charges are being made." Since it was the first time the third judge had spoken, everyone looked at her. She was a handsome woman and her dark tan (hunting in the Shires, yachting in the Med and the Bahamas) contrasted effectively with the white linen suit she was wearing this afternoon. It was clear she didn't like Carlos de Sevile, but it was also well-known that she never permitted personal feelings to influence her in any way.

"Very well," Carlos said recklessly. In the brief conversation he had had with his almost hysterical assistant, he had gathered that Lauren's show had been a greater success than Carlos's own, that Michael Landrill had been there with a huge party, and that the destruction of most of her costumes had been used as a sympathy-getter. Something needed to be done. He said, "My assistant, Dicky Devon, will bring a written statement to the cruise director's office within twenty minutes."

Lady Winston-Bell spoke up. "I have read the rules quite carefully. I assure you there is nothing stated therein that denies the designer the right to present his or her work in any way he or she deems suitable."

Reb Crowell glanced around. They had an audience, dozens of well-dressed men and women obviously enjoying the drama of this confrontation. The reporter suggested, "Why don't we call a conference in the cruise director's office? Request all the designers, including Mrs. Rose, to attend? Better to clear this up right away."

Lady Winston-Bell and Mrs. Cornelius nodded. Carlos, neglecting to thank them for their consideration, hurried away to lobby with as many of the designers as he could reach before the meeting.

Lauren stood quietly backstage, surrounded by her appalled team. No one knew quite what to say. After a moment, Lauren broke the silence. "Well, at least I'm to be given a fair hearing, which is more than the wine-thrower gave me."

Derek touched her shoulder lightly. "May I come with you? You might need some support."

Lauren placed her hand lightly over his for a moment. "Thank you. But I have an idea this inquisition is to be limited to designers and judges."

Violet nodded her head sharply once. "We'll wait outside in the lobby, luv. Then you can shout for us if you want us."

Lauren took time to check her appearance in a ladies lounge before she went to Maida's office. When she got there, she glanced around the outer lobby hopefully. Just a glimpse of Mike's big, comforting body would have given her support for the coming ordeal. Violet and Derek were there, seated in two leather armchairs, and they gave her encouraging smiles. Mike wasn't there.

Inside the office, Maida was listening while Reb Crowell reviewed the situation. Mrs. Cornelius and Lady Winston-Bell were talking quietly at one side of the room. Stewards were bringing in extra chairs. Several of the designers were already present. Maida, looking harried, asked the stewards to bring tea. Lauren, feeling like a criminal, took a seat by herself near the door. Jan Haliday, the designer behind the Janus line, entered, noticed Lauren, and came to sit beside her.

"I caught your show," he said, smiling. "It was awesome, when you consider what de Sevile did to your collection."

"Thank you," Lauren answered, more cheered than she realized by this friendly gesture. "Your show was, uh, awesome, too. Those leathers are wonderful. How—?"

Still smiling, Jan shook his head. "Trade secret, Mrs. Rose," he murmured.

Lauren frowned. "You said de Sevile wrecked my costumes. Do you *know* that for a fact?"

Jan stopped smiling. "No, dear. I just took it for granted. He's such a nasty little beast and that's just the sort of thing he'd do. He's been bad-mouthing you, both personally and as a designer, ever since he came on board. The rest of us can't quite understand it." His raised eyebrows were a request for information.

Lauren said slowly, "I think he may be worried because Landrill's, to whom he's under contract, has made me an offer. His contract is up next year and I'm informed they don't intend to renew."

Jan whistled softly. "That would do it. Have you any evidence Carlos's boys were near your stateroom?"

"No. And I'm not sure it was Carlos. There's someone else who wants to manipulate my business and he had a better chance than anyone to get into my cabin." She caught herself up and stared hard into the handsome face beside her. "You must have magic," she said. "I can't think why I'm telling you all my problems like this."

"Maybe because we're not rivals," Jan suggested, smiling widely. "I make a rather good friend, in spite of what creatures like de Sevile have to say about me." He stared at her worried face. "I'll vote for you, dear." He laughed. "Anything to frustrate our darling Carlos."

Lauren felt comforted but her musings were cut short abruptly when several people entered the office at once. When they were seated, Maida took the floor. She explained briefly the reason for the meeting and told the designers that there would be a chance for each one to express an opinion, if so desired, and then a vote would be taken as to whether Lauren Rose's presentation had in any way broken the letter or the spirit of the Fashion Cruise agreement.

Carlos was on his feet at once, spouting his objections.

Maida held up one hand. "Señor de Sevile," she said quietly, "you are aware that you have only one chance to speak at this meeting? After that you may vote, but you must not speak again."

"This is absurd," he shrilled. "I am not obliged to conform to your ridiculous rules—" He stopped, made aware of what he had said by the quizzical smiles of the other designers and Reb Crowell's wolfish grin.

The reporter made the too-obvious point. "You're telling us, *Señor* Carlos, that Mrs. Rose has to abide by the rules and you don't?"

Carlos sat down, for once aware that he was in hostile territory, not surrounded by his usual sycophants.

Maida went on as though the interruption had not occurred. "I'll poll each designer. Then I'll ask the judges for their opinion. Mrs. Rose, you won't have a vote."

Lauren smiled. "I understand."

Briefly and succinctly, Maida outlined the problem. She began, however, with a brief description of the sabotage. As an unexpected bit of evidence, she pressed a bell and a steward wheeled in the rack of ruined garments. Everyone stared, appalled, at the reeking mess. Designers themselves, they knew all too well the endless hours that had gone into creating such a collection; anger and disgust were plain on most of the faces. Adah Shere presented her habitual serenely blank expression. Maartens was frowning slightly but not revealing his thoughts.

Carlos got up to speak, met Maida's glance, and sat

down. It was obvious, however, that he did not feel this display of sodden garments had much to do with Lauren's performance.

Then, after the steward had wheeled the rack out, Maida continued, "Mrs. Rose's presentation was dance— quite permissible and even rather universally accepted as routine by most designers—and some mime to illustrate the little story she devised to show her costumes to best effect."

Carlos could no longer contain himself. "*Little story*! It was a half-hour show!"

"What would you have done, de Sevile," drawled Maartens, "if someone had ruined all your costumes just hours before your show?"

"I wouldn't permit such a stupid thing to happen to me," Carlos scoffed. "I'm a professional, not some two-bit dressmaker!"

"That finishes your right to comment," Maida said sternly. "I want to hear from the other designers. Have any of you a comment to make before we take the vote?"

"Since I didn't see the show," Telford said, "I really can't make a fair comment."

"I did see it," Jan spoke up. "It was bright, effective in showing off the mobility of the dresses and the feminine styling, witty, and in good taste." He grinned at de Sevile.

Maida passed out the slips of paper and pencils. "Please write yes if you wish to allow Mrs. Rose's presentation to be admitted; no if you wish to disallow it."

When they had written, Maida collected the slips. Of the six who voted, three were yes, the other three no.

"Tie vote," Maida announced formally. "This means the three judges will have to vote to break the tie." She handed slips to the judges.

Lady Winston-Bell said firmly, "I'm going to vote *viva voce*. My decision is that Mrs. Rose's innovative-through-dire-necessity presentation should be admitted to the contest."

"I'm afraid I disagree," Mrs. Cornelius said. "We really shouldn't open the door to Hollywood-type performances in a fashion show. I vote no."

Lauren's heart fell. For a brief moment, she had felt a lifting of the heart at the firm support of Lady Winston-Bell. Now she was back where she started. Would Rebel Crowell want to spoil his story? Lauren could see the headline? *Noted designer kicked out of posh Fashion Show on board luxury liner Queen Elizabeth II.*

Reb didn't even look at her. "I vote yes." That was it.

Lauren rose quickly and almost ran from the room. She was deeply afraid that if she tried to thank her friends—and she wasn't sure after the secret ballot who her friends were—she would probably break into tears and embarrass everyone. Also she couldn't face Carlos's fierce glare or bear to listen to any more of his disparaging remarks. Her show was still part of the contest, but at this point Lauren didn't really care who would win it. She was pretty sure it wouldn't be herself. How could it, with only a third of her costumes available for judging? They didn't really know what the other dresses and suits and the rest had looked like. But at least she wasn't thrown out, like some sort of pushy impostor. She hurried to her stateroom, anxious to rest and recover her poise in private.

And somewhere in her mind was the hope that Mike Landrill might be there to meet her: Mike, who had brought guests to her showing, to fill the seats and give it a popular, successful ambience.

Chapter Seven

❧

Lauren and her models dressed for dinner in an atmosphere of mingled triumph and fear. Lauren was fighting the depression that had enveloped her as the afternoon waned and Mike didn't put in an appearance. Dani was high on the excitement of the favorable vote for their show. When Lauren told her they had made it only by one vote, she grinned and said, "One's as good as a hundred, if it's in our favor." Nella was nervous again, audibly wondering what else Carlos or Herbert had up their sleeves.

"Maybe we shouldn't eat or drink anything tonight, Lauren," she suggested.

"Do you see Carlos or Herbert as Borgias?" Lauren teased. At Nella's frightened stare, she added quickly, "Just a joke, Nella. Neither of them has access to the kitchens and I'd stake my life on the integrity of the *Queen*'s stewards."

"You might have to," Nella muttered.

However, when they were all three dressed and ready, a more cheerful atmosphere prevailed. There is nothing, thought Lauren, so reassuring to a woman as a beautiful dress that flatters her.

They did look impressive, she decided, casting a critical eye over Dani in the jewel, Nella in her bronze silk, and her own image in the mirror. She was wearing the

dress Mike had taken off her that night—was it only
Tuesday, *two* nights ago? Its alluring caftan of sheer
chiffon, with the sensuously tight bodice of shimmering
sequins beneath, had attracted his admiration then.
Would he see her, want her, tonight?

It was a quarter to eight, and the Captain's Dinner
was set for eight, to be followed by the awards ceremony.

"Will we do, Lauren?" Nella asked.

Lauren said proudly, "You are beautiful."

Both models smiled. Then they held up their heads
and strolled along the passage and into the elevator as
though they were on the runway. Lauren's heart lifted.
Whatever anyone said, whether they won or lost, they'd
put up a good show.

The plan was that all the designers and their models
were to meet in the captain's dayroom for cocktails before
dinner. The judges would be there also, and Maida and
several officers. A few special guests had also been
invited. Lauren hoped one would be Mike. Then, after
cocktails, the party would proceed to the Queen's Grill
for dinner. Following that, they would adjourn to the
theater, where an audience of interested fashion-lovers
would be waiting for the awards ceremonies.

These were to include a showing of each designer's
choice of two best costumes while the designer commented, if he or she wished, from one side of the stage.
The judges' decision would then be announced, and
prizes awarded. It seemed there were to be more prizes
than one. As a special feature, the awards ceremony
would be broadcast to all lounges and even into those
cabins that had television as part of the regular fur-
nishing. This hopeful gesture was to avoid crowding in
the theater.

"Some hope," was Dani's show-wise comment.

It didn't take Lauren long to find the big man with

he wide shoulders. He stood out for many reasons.
he and her models were greeted by junior officers and
ed at once to where the captain was chatting with Lady
Vinston-Bell and Maida Hass. The captain welcomed
he three women with pleasantly correct compliments
n their appearance and a glinting aside that of course
ie mustn't show favoritism. Her Ladyship was gracious
nd friendly as ever. The three were passed deftly to
Maida, who took them to the buffet and asked their
preferences in drinks.

Her eyebrows lifted a fraction as all three chose
Perrier. "Keeping a clear head? Perhaps that's wise,"
he murmured, gesturing toward the center of the
layroom, where Carlos was holding forth with a whis-
key in one fist.

"Don't look so frightened, Nella," Dani teased. "He
can't eat you in front of all these people. You're not on
he menu."

"I guess we aren't on the prize list, either," Nella
mourned. They all glanced around. The room was
ammed with gorgeously dressed women. Diamonds,
emeralds, rubies, and lesser gems shimmered on every
surface, Lauren thought wryly. They'd hang them from
their noses if it didn't hurt. The men were equally
festive, with some pretty wild jackets on display for this
fashion-conscious group. It's as though they wanted to
rival the models, Lauren confided to Dani.

"Most of them'd have to lose about thirty pounds
before they'd be competition," snipped the model.

And then he was beside her. She sensed more than
felt his broad shoulders and his silver-gray eyes. Lauren
didn't care how revealing her expression was. She was
so happy to see him.

His rather anxious expression softened into a wicked
grin. He bent close to her and said in her ear, "Not

here, darling. You're going to have to wait until we ge
to my cabin."

Lauren felt the warm blood rising in her cheeks. Y
gods, she mocked herself, I'm an adult and this guy ca
make me blush. But she didn't care, because the show
was safely over, and Mike was here beside her. Wha
could go wrong?

Mike was saying, "I heard over the grapevine tha
your show was allowed, in spite of the theatrical format."

Lauren nodded, smiling. "I didn't let anyone down."

Mike frowned. "I also hear that for some reason
probably her loyalty to Maartens, Claire Cornelius i:
claiming that you mustn't be considered a serious con
tender because you didn't show enough costumes."

"I'm sorry she feels that way. But, then, she's right
isn't she?" Lauren knew she would feel deeply hur
later, but right now just being with concerned an(
attentive Mike was pleasure enough.

"Are you being a good sport or are you just punch
drunk after the session in Maida's office?" Mike askec
in a louder voice.

Dani spoke up unexpectedly. "I think she's in love,'
the model teased. "Better watch out she doesn't miss
her footing and fall overboard."

They all laughed except Nella, who hadn't got the
point and looked at Lauren with a worried frown.

Several couples and some unescorted women moved
in on Mike, who was evidently well-known and liked.
He introduced Lauren and the models, even draping
one arm lightly over Lauren's shoulders. The socialites
tended to ignore her. Some of them quizzed the models.
Dani made them laugh with her spirited plain-speaking.
The men tended to stare at Nella, who always looked
serenely lovely and rather mysterious when she was on
display, as she was now.

Ben Nowak strolled over and Preppy Telford joined him. The male designers were definitely patronizing to Lauren; both mentioned that they hadn't seen her show but had heard it was unusual.

Damned with this faint praise, Lauren was holding her tongue with a feeling of mounting annoyance when Mike said it for her.

"I saw the whole show. So did Buffy and her crowd. Ask them. It was really terrific. The least boring fashion show I've ever attended."

He got some hard looks for that one, but Lauren knew that the designers, no matter how powerful with their own cliques, would hardly wish to cross swords with a man of Landrill's importance and wealth. They drifted away.

"Nice cutthroat business you're in," Mike muttered. "Let's eat."

Fortunately for protocol, the captain had apparently had the same idea and he led his guests down to the Queen's Grill. Lauren had been placed at a table of only medium visibility; there weren't any bad tables in the Queen's Grill, but she wasn't near the head table by any means.

Mike followed while the steward led her to it. He frowned. It was a table for four. The other three seats were occupied by Jan, his partner, Sidney, and a bright-eyed youth in a magnificent ruby velvet dinner jacket with a matching cummerbund.

"I'll toss you for that seat," Mike drawled.

"But I specially requested to be seated with Janus," protested the youth.

Mike turned to the steward. "Where's my table? Landrill's the name."

"If you'll come with me, sir?"

Mike gripped Lauren's elbow, grinned insouciantly at the smiling Jan, and followed the steward.

Lauren said, "Really, Mike, I don't mind. Jan was very supportive today in Maida's office. And he voted to accept my presentation."

"Bully for him," Mike said shortly. "Now we're going to find a table. I'm hungry, what with all this temperament and jostling for position. I've a good mind to eat in my own suite."

"I need to be here, Mike," Lauren said.

He glared at her. "Of course you do. Being part of this ridiculous rat race or Fashion Cruise or whatever you call it. I can tell you what I call it." He pronounced a rather crude epithet.

Lauren chuckled. "Don't let Carlos hear you," she advised.

"You think he'd challenge me to a duel?" Mike grinned hopefully. "Needles at forty paces?"

"You're talking about Landrill's prize designer," Lauren teased.

Mike groaned. "Don't remind me."

By this time the steward had brought them to the kindly guidance of the maître d'. That suave and charming gentleman discovered that Mike had been assigned to a table for eight, and that Buffy Landrill was his partner.

"Is she here yet? She's usually late—likes to make a grand entrance."

The maître d' consulted his list. "Mrs. Landrill has not yet been shown to her table," he admitted.

Mike gave him a conspiratorial grin. "Mrs. Landrill is my sister-in-law. I'd like to arrange a little treat for her. She's very eager to be seated with one of the seven stars of the show. Mrs. Rose has graciously agreed to relinquish her place at Janus's table so Mrs. Landrill may sit there."

The maître d' gave him an avuncular glance. "Is that so, sir?" he asked.

"Indeed it is. Oh, here she comes now. I'll explain it to her." Mike strode over to the doorway where Buffy, looking petulant, was hovering. He talked rapidly. Her expression went from surprise to suspicion to delight. Mike led her toward the waiting maître d'.

"You mean *Janus* actually requested that I sit at his table?" she was saying.

The maître d' smiled. "Let me escort you there, Mrs. Landrill," he said with charm and authority.

Buffy giggled and followed him without a glance at Mike or Lauren.

"Very neat, sir," the steward murmured, leading Lauren and Mike to a table near the captain's.

"How could you?" whispered Lauren.

"Silence," Mike warned. "Never admit anything." He had cupped a warm hand around her elbow again. Lauren would have followed him anywhere.

When they reached the table, they found it already occupied except for the two seats originally intended for Buffy and Mike. Everyone wanted to know where Buffy was, although they smiled pleasantly enough at Lauren when Mike introduced her.

"Buffy," Mike said portentously, "has been requisitioned to keep Janus happy."

There was a blank silence and then laughter.

"No, really?" asked Tippy, a husky blonde from Buffy's Hunt Club. "Hadn't realized Buff was into leather."

This brought another laugh, and Mike seated Lauren. The man next to her smiled and said, "Are you from California, Laurie?"

Lauren resisted the temptation to correct him, and smiled sweetly. "I'm with September Song."

Her neighbor moved a little closer. "A model." He looked her over avidly. "Isn't Mike the lucky one."

Lauren laughed. She couldn't help it; the whole setup seemed childish, somehow. "I'm Lauren Rose, the designer. My show was this afternoon. I'm sure you didn't see it; I would have remembered your face." I can play these games, too, she decided. She grinned at the surprise and pleasure on his face.

"Designer?" he said. Clearly, he'd never heard of her.

The woman next to him had been listening. She gave Lauren a condescending smile. "September Song, did you say? Do you design sportswear?"

Suddenly Mike's dark, velvet voice sounded so close to Lauren's ear that her nerves quivered. "September Song is the newest thing in the fashion world," he told the woman. "Landrill's has been trying to get Lauren under contract for several years. Wish me luck, Baba."

Baba, Tippy, and Midge turned as one person to stare at Lauren. If Landrill's was after her, their glances seemed to say, there must be more to her than they had thought. Lauren's smile was wry. Was that all it took? She glanced at Mike, caught the glint in his eye, and realized that he knew exactly what he was doing. Suddenly she felt lighthearted, happy, mischievous.

"I haven't signed yet," she said, trying hard for the prep-school accent. "My designs aren't for just everybody."

A rapacious light entered the women's eyes. Lauren could tell they were kicking themselves for not taking in her show. "September Song?" Midge pondered. "I haven't heard—"

"Of course you haven't," Lauren said cordially. "I really don't have to advertise."

This statement had them all watching her with heightened interest. Tippy said rather too loudly, "Oh, you're a cult designer, like Janus!"

Lauren laughed lightly. "Quite unlike Janus, actually."

Mike took control. "I can't let you tease these people, Lauren. September Song, which will be featured in its own elegant boutiques throughout the Landrill chain, is for the woman who, like the finest wines, has matured enough to please the connoisseur in man—, the man of discerning taste. Of course, it's caviar to the general public. They can't afford it and they don't see its special appeal. Now can't we talk about something else? How many laps of the pool did you swim today, Midge? Or did you spend all your time in the Golden Door, being massaged?"

This started a spate of small talk about the skeet-shooting, yoga, and dance exercise, with the men boasting about their wins at the Players Club. But Lauren noticed that the three women were casting speculative glances her way. She was glad she was wearing the Sultan's Dream.

By the time the sweets tray was being offered, Lauren was beginning to feel nervous again. She wondered if Dani and Nella, dining with all the other models, were enjoying the meal or worrying about the awards presentation. Dani could hold her own, and some of the models were very pleasant people, but Nella tended to get fearful in a challenging situation.

Mike was reading her expression again. He leaned close to her and whispered, "Would you like to go to the theater now? I think the other designers may wish to head that way very soon, so it won't make you look unsure of yourself."

He thought of everything. Lauren was so besotted with the man that she was ready to accept anything he said. She nodded gratefully. "I'd really like to be there, Mike."

He nodded, glanced around the table, and got up. "Lauren's got to check on her models. We'll see you all later."

"Mike, you aren't leaving us now," protested Baba, who had hardly taken her eyes off him since he sat down at the table.

" 'Fraid so, honey," Mike drawled. "I can't let this genius get out of my sight. The other stores have scouts everywhere." He laughed as he led a smiling Lauren away.

As he left her at the entrance to the theater, Mike looked at Lauren intently. "Have you got it together?"

She nodded. "I think so. And thank you for your support."

"Think nothing of it." He grinned suddenly. "I'm already planning exactly what my fee will be." And he gave her a rakish leer.

Lauren couldn't help laughing. His look of satisfaction told her that was exactly what he had hoped for.

The mood in the waiting room off the theater was tense and edgy. Carlos, with two of his assistants beside him, glowered at Lauren fiercely once and then ignored her. He was chain-smoking, with imminent danger to his models' costumes. He'd chosen to feature two of the most strident in color and style, and Lauren felt a secret pleasure in his poor judgment. Still, she chided herself, perhaps the audience would enjoy purple and crimson and black with a trim of white bobbles.

Maartens had a pleasant smile for her. He was obviously a gentleman, gray-haired, with a good tan and a trim body. Lauren thought he was about sixty, but it really was hard to tell. Jan Haliday nodded and grinned, shaking his head over the trick Mike had played at dinner, but he didn't approach her to talk. In fact, very few conversations were heard. Most of the designers

alked only to their own models, with brief, last-minute
nstructions. Lauren didn't have anything to say to her
wo. They knew the routine better than she did, and
hey knew what Derek had planned.

Lauren had a sudden horrible thought. What if the
udges disqualified her collection when they found out
what Derek and she had planned with Tony? Oh, well,
she tried to comfort herself, I'll never win with Mrs.
Cornelius against me anyway. And Mike has agreed to
hire me as a Landrill's designer, so I guess I'm safe
financially. Somehow it wasn't completely satisfying, but
it would have to do.

She went to the peephole. The theater was packed.
The TV crews were fussing around, getting in everyone's
way. There was a hubbub of voices, laughter, calls from
one group to another—a carnival atmosphere that surprised Lauren. Then the audience fell silent as the
captain led Lady Winston-Bell to the stage, while Mike
escorted Mrs. Cornelius and Maida led Reb Crowell to
the judges' table in front of the stage.

The captain introduced Lady Winston-Bell, and then
added, "We are very grateful to Sir George for permit-
ting us to monopolize so much of his wife's time during
this voyage. I only hope he will forgive us when he
hears how grateful we all are for his forbearance."

The applause, of course, was appropriately loud. Then
the captain introduced the other two judges to equal
applause. The house lights lowered, spotlights and flood-
lights played on the stage, and Lady Winston-Bell began to introduce the designers. She called them in the
order in which they had made their original presentations. As each designer came forward, he introduced
his own best designs worn by two of his models.

The audience had evidently dined well and wined
better, as the applause was generous for everyone. By

the time Lauren's name was called, she was wondering if anyone would have the energy to clap even once more. She was surprised at the enthusiastic reception she got. She called her models by name; they deserved that bit of recognition. The two women paraded across the stage and then took up positions at the rear.

Suddenly there was a titter of laughter from the audience. Those who had seen the show waited, smiling, for the reaction of their friends who hadn't. The cause of their mirth was a cleaning woman who had wandered in from the side of the stage and now paused to examine the bronze silk costume. Polly and Dolly rushed in, dressed as stewardesses who had been sent to remove the intruder. Someone in the audience hooted. The twins held a sheet in front of Violet and Nella. When they took it away, Violet was wearing the bronze silk and Nella, wearing Violet's clothes, was carried off the stage by Polly and Dolly.

Derek, distinguished in formal evening wear, came on stage and bowed to Violet. A soft Viennese waltz sounded from back stage, then went smoothly into "The Anniversary Waltz" as the graceful couple began to dance. They went around the stage once. Then Derek, holding Violet closer, gave her a brief, tender kiss. The audience, caught up in the unexpected romantic interlude, began to clap as Derek waltzed Violet offstage.

Lady Winston-Bell rose and called everyone to order. "Now that you have seen a sampling of the beautiful, charming, or striking designs that the seven finest American designers have offered for our enjoyment this week, your judges are ready to announce the winners, two designers whose true elegance of line, forward-looking styles, and suitability for their clients' life-style have most impressed us. Each of the two is to receive a golden plaque, engraved with the words: *Queen Eliza-*

beth II Fashion Cruise Award for Elegance in Design. I call on Madame Adah Shere and Mr. Ian Maartens."

There was thunderous applause as Maartens escorted Madame Shere to the stage, where Lady Winston-Bell presented the awards. Maartens spoke a few words of acknowledgment for them both. When they had left the stage, to continuing applause, Lady Winston-Bell held up one hand for silence.

"The judges have decided that one more award can and should be made. The Cunard Line, represented by their cruise director, Miss Maida Hass, has graciously agreed to grant a special award, for suitability for its clients, creativity, panache in presentation, and courage under stress; the Queen's Golden Award, to Mrs. Lauren Rose, September Song."

The applause was sincere and hearty.

Mike came on stage to lead Lauren toward Lady Winston-Bell to receive her award. It was a golden heart on a slim gold chain. He offered her his arm and she was surprised and touched to see that he had tied a violet silk scarf, one of her signature items, around his sleeve. He intended to escort her offstage to accept the congratulations of the audience, as Maartens had done for Madame Shere, but he was caught by the incredulous joy on Lauren's face. He stood looking down at her for a moment. She looked back at him, the love she felt for him plainly visible in her glowing eyes and soft mouth. Suddenly ignoring the delighted audience, Mike swept her into his arms and kissed her.

Laughter and applause.

Then Lady Winston-Bell announced, "If *that* is what happens when one wears a September Song dress, I intend to buy nothing else."

Sir George rose to salute her from the audience.

"Hear! Hear!" he called to her, smiling. This brought down the house.

When he finally got Lauren away from well-wishers—among whom Carlos and Herbert were significantly missing—Mike led her firmly to his suite. Lauren sat down on the chair, still stunned. The man grinned as he poured her sherry. "Drink this. The show is over and it won't matter if you get a little mellow."

Lauren accepted it without comment, and drank it down.

"You can have one more, and then I have another relaxing therapy in mind for you."

Lauren smiled up at him. "You were right, you know. What we have—what I feel for you," she corrected herself, "is too special to be spoiled by bargaining. Being commercial, you called it."

Mike's eyebrows rose. "You mean you aren't holding out for marriage?" He was sorry as soon as the words left his lips; surprise had caused him to say what sounded crudely offensive at this point. He stared at Lauren apprehensively. "I shouldn't have said that. I'm sorry."

"But you were right. I think we both have a lot to learn about love. And I want to learn it with you."

Mike came to her swiftly, a man of experience and passion, but with almost a youthful look of delight and anticipation on his face. He swung her into his arms and carried her to his bedroom. There, he set her on her feet beside his bed and went back to lock the door.

"Nothing is going to interrupt us now," he whispered as he came back and drew her into his arms. "I love this dress on you, but, darling, I think I'll love it better off." And he began, with big hands that trembled just a little, to undo the glittering, small collar and remove the caftan.

Sensing his need, Lauren didn't try to help in his

task. Very soon he had her before him in the two scraps of satin and lace that were her only other garments. Hose and dress were flung aside casually, but Lauren didn't object. The dress had indeed served its purpose, bringing her where she most wished to be, into Mike's arms. His hands were gentle on her body. Then they stilled, and he lifted his eyes to hers. Soberly he placed her on the bed.

"I want to take off my clothes now. It isn't fair that I'm still dressed."

As he quickly disrobed, Lauren wondered at the sensitivity this man was learning to show. That he should stop to think of her feelings, when he so evidently wanted and needed her. She leaned up and helped him undo the well-fitting dress trousers. She heard his breath catch in a gasp.

She looked up quickly. It was all there in his face, the need, the passion, the pleasure. She went on with her task. In a few minutes he was beside her on the bed.

"Are you comfortable? Too cold?" he asked, warmly possessive.

She put her arms around his neck. "I'm comfortable." It didn't seem necessary to make any speeches. He was here; she was with him, where she passionately wished to be. She loved him better than anyone or anything she had ever known. Lauren kissed his lips with sweetness and desire.

Their coming together had a richness, a total involvement of bodies and, somehow, minds. Each was luxuriating in the other's sensuous lovemaking, but in both their minds was a wish to provide an equally wonderful stimulation for the other. Soon Mike was roused and uttering small groans deep in his throat. Yet still he controlled his desire and worked with hands and mouth to give Lauren a rising joy. When she was clutching his shoulders with frantic fingers, he entered her and, thrusting eagerly, brought them both to ecstatic climax.

Lauren cried out, and Mike held her closer, gasping his pleasure.

Afterward, as they lay together, bodies touching, Lauren sighed deeply in perfect content. She stroked him lightly from his shoulder to his navel. "That was wonderful," she said softly. "You were wonderful."

"I know." Mike grinned complacently down at her averted face, which was resting on his chest. He was obviously enjoying the soothing motion of her hand, for he caught it and directed it lower. Then, as she willingly took up his suggestion, he hugged her and patted her round bottom.

"You're a comfortable little woman, you know that?" He missed Lauren's unobtrusive stiffening against the rather patronizing gesture and comment because he was hugging her again, painfully hard. He got out of bed, stretching unselfconsciously. Lauren couldn't keep her eyes off his hard, brown body, loving the long muscled legs and thighs, the taut stomach, the broad shoulders.

He caught her scrutiny and laughed. "I like the way you look, too, honey—very sexy and well-loved. I'm going to take a shower and order us some food and coffee. Care to join me?"

Lauren was tempted, but she felt vaguely uneasy. The street phrase "coming down from a high," occurred to her briefly. She shook her head and tried for a smile. "I'll wait."

He grinned down at her possessively. "Come on and try it." He pulled her out of the bed and into his arms. "Relax. I know that you don't like one-, or two-, or even three-night stands or shipboard romances, you told me so. But this is different. This is Mike and Lauren. We've got something good going here."

Lauren couldn't face his smile. "I thought I knew who I was and what I wanted. I've learned that anyone can change. *I* can change, grow. You've told me what you *don't* want, Mike. I understand, believe me. We're all of us what life has made us. But we do change and grow, and learn what makes us tick."

She faced his suddenly intent, hard look honestly. "I . . . I enjoy whatever this is we have together, Mike. But what I'm learning is that when I love, I have to trust and give. It's that simple. Perhaps I'm not exactly comfortable with it yet—it's a new way for me—but I'm walking it. Have patience with my stumbling." She caught her breath at the warm look she glimpsed in his eyes. He said nothing, so Lauren went on, "So all right! No promises from either of us, no binding commitments. I thank you for your gift of your . . . affection, may I call it? No, your term last night was 'lovely lust.' I'll accept that."

"Will you?" Mike asked somberly, putting her away from him. He got a robe from the closet and thrust his arms into it. As he was tying the cord, he watched her, her shapely body posed so forlornly against the bed, so vulnerable. "Somehow I don't think you'll be very comfortable with several years of lust, even if it is lovely. I'm sure you want a hell of a lot more than that. I think you want all a man could ever give you of passion and sharing and—to coin a phrase—true love." He grinned wryly, mocking himself as much as her. "I also think you talk too much. It tends to dilute the mixture."

Catching her startled, anxious look, he smiled more easily. "Oh, you've hooked me, Lauren Rose. I know I'm going to get trouble along with you, woman, but I'm going to hold on to you. Because you're loving and sexy and sweet and insatiable and everything I really enjoy, all wrapped into one lovely little package." He came to her again, shucking off his robe and taking her close against his warm, hard body.

"We both need a shower for more reasons than cleanliness. I'll bet you've never taken a shower with a man before, hmm?" She shook her head, no. He hugged her briefly, then let her go. "We'll talk first; settle details. I hate silly distractions when I'm having a really creative shower." His grin asked her to share the fun with him. Loving him, Lauren beamed back.

He took a deep breath. "Well, then. We'll be docking tomorrow at Southampton. It's not likely we'll get much chance to talk privately. All those British Press lads will be clustering around you, the winner of the Golden Heart! So we've got to settle our business tonight."

He knew at once that Lauren didn't like the sound of that word. Her face was turned toward his, as open as a flower, as vulnerable. He said briskly, "What hotel are you booked into?"

"The Bristol."

Mike frowned. "I'd sooner have you with me at the Ritz. I'll speak to the purser in the morning and have you transferred there. I think I have a two-bedroom suite booked."

"Dani and Nella and I are flying back to Los Angeles Sunday afternoon," Lauren told him.

He frowned. "You're not worried that two grown women might get lost in London, are you? I promise you they don't need Mommy to shepherd them onto the plane."

"You *have* met Nella?" Lauren gibed. "After all, they're my responsibility."

"All right, then," he gave in. "I'll send a car to pick them up and get them out to Heathrow. I'll even instruct the driver to make sure they get on the plane.

You and I, lady, have more important matters to attend to. Beginning right now."

Lauren looked up into his face, alight with laughter and male virility. Everything about him seemed to be glowing, sparkling, crackling with electricity. She could hardly draw her gaze from his eyes, silver in their frame of thick black lashes, wooing her, dominating her.

To protect herself, she teased, "Better have that shower right now, buster. You need to cool off." She sidestepped his mock-predatory advance. "I'll just slip along to my stateroom and get some rest. You've reminded me of my responsibilities."

"Not without your massage," Mike said complacently.

"*Massage,*" Lauren almost squeaked. What was this wild man up to now? "I thought it was a shower."

"Massage," Mike reiterated firmly. "Kindly old Doc Michael is advising you that a massage with liquid soap is one of the truly satisfying experiences in life. Properly applied, that stuff turns ordinary skin into satin. What it will do to *your* silky epidermis boggles my mind. You're going to let me show you, aren't you? For therapeutic reasons only, of course," he coaxed, eyes and smile seductive.

Lauren felt the warm color glowing in her face. Surely a professional woman wasn't blushing? His knowing grin proved that she was.

"Please let me show you how relaxing a massage can be, Lauren? I promise you, all your troubles will flow away with the soapsuds. Trust me."

A few minutes later, Lauren told Mike, "This could easily get to be one of my favorite activities!"

Her body felt as though it were purring. Mike was rubbing her back with liquid soap, massaging so firmly with both hands that she was forced to steady herself against the shower wall. He was right, the devil! The soap was fragrantly seductive, making her skin silk-and-satin beneath his fingers. With the steamy warmth and his overwhelming presence, she felt swept away to a world of pleasure she had only glimpsed at before.

He turned her to face him with soapy, insistent fingers. At first he only pulled her closer while he washed and kneaded her from shoulders to thighs. And then his touch became lighter, more provocative. He lifted her chin, so that her swelling lips were just inches below his. As he kissed her, he lifted her body firmly against his and entered her in a smooth motion of pure joining. They surged together, melded into one by the water streaming down their faces and searching out the crevices left between their passionately entwined bodies. Lauren's ecstasy was both a flight of freedom and pleasure and a discovery of a surer, happier self she knew only Mike could have taught her was there.

Afterward, instead of separating, Mike continued to hold her up closely against his chest.

"Wet and soapy," Lauren mocked, not daring to let him see how vulnerable she was to his splendid masculinity. She lifted her head to laugh at him. It was her undoing.

Mike responded quickly, moving his shoulders and exposing her to the direct spurt of the water. As she gasped and held her face against his broad chest, he said, "That will teach you. We're not just wet and soapy, you little nut. We're together, linked, joined." He held her close with both hands supporting her rounded buttocks.

Lauren rubbed her wet face against his equally wet chest. "Let's get out. I think I'm drowning."

"I haven't finished my work," Mike said airily. "You'll have to hold on to me, I need both hands."

He got some more of the soap and massaged it luxuriously over her shoulders, down her back, then over her rounded breasts. It was sleek and slippery, fragrant and utterly sensuous. Drugged with pleasure, Lauren mused, This can't be lust. Lust means seeking your own gratification at the expense of your partner, doesn't it? This man is working for my satisfaction, my pleasure. This is . . .

But she didn't finish the thought, for Mike had again begun a slow, loving thrusting that brought her whole body to life. . . .

Trust him? Lauren thought as she lazily brushed her hair half an hour later. He's taught me more about love's tenderness, love's unselfishness, love's melting sweetness, in three days than I learned in all the years of my marriage. Alone in the bathroom, drying herself after the shower, she moved in a languid dream state, mind and body relaxed and glowing.

Mike.

She hadn't known that any man could be at the same time so strong, so ardent, so gentle—and so funny. As she remembered his jokes, her lips curved into a smile. He took a boyish delight in her pleasure, her amusement. Lauren realized with a little pang of guilt that his whole attention had been focused on her satisfaction rather than his own. She had responded passionately, true, but all the creativity in loving had been his.

Frowning, Lauren stared at the reflection of her face in the faintly steamy mirror. Then she pulled on a blue velour robe that was hanging on the hook behind the door. She'd get her clothes, dress, and go back to her own stateroom at once. Otherwise, she was likely to make a fool of herself, adoring him.

Chapter Eight

Mike refused to let Lauren return to her own cabin. When the steward brought the trolley with Welsh rabbit, fruits in whipped cream, and coffee, Lauren retired hastily to the bathroom, clutching her clothing. A few minutes later Mike tapped lightly on the door.

"You can come out now," he teased. "We are alone at last."

Lauren came out of the bathroom with a languid aplomb that Dani would have envied. She had put on just her lacy briefs and the chiffon caftan. She posed in the doorway, miming a movie vamp.

Mike whistled appreciatively. "I can see I'm never going to have a dull moment." He grinned. "I hope I can measure up."

For some reason this caused Lauren to dissolve into gales of laughter. After a moment, Mike joined her.

"Well, I can't say it isn't fun to laugh together," he admitted a few minutes later, reluctant to see the passionate awareness dissipated.

"The family that laughs together—" Lauren began, and then halted in mortification. She hadn't meant to bring that particular idea up ever again. She'd have to watch her tongue.

Again Mike seemed able to read her mind. "No, don't set limits on the things you say, Lauren. I want you to be yourself." He suddenly turned on a pompous, lecturing manner. "The Lauren Rose I met and fell in love with on the greatest liner afloat."

Lauren was so delighted with the phrase "fell in love with" that she turned to the food, laughing, and suggested, "Let's eat and build up our strength for those paparazzi you said would hit us in the morning."

As they filled their plates, Lauren noticed that Mike had a rather abstracted air. Had it been the mention of the newspaper reporters who might pester him? Considering his prominence and wealth, it hardly seemed likely. He would have developed techniques, surely, to deal with such problems. Perhaps he was suddenly uncomfortable with the kind of commitment that was developing between himself and Lauren?

She didn't try to ignore the challenge such a man as Michael Landrill presented. He was hard to handle. No woman would ever really tame him, but, oh, she loved him for the difficult, suspicious, cynical man he was. He enjoyed women, that was plain. He was an inventive and ardent lover. But he wouldn't allow himself to trust a woman, after what he had seen and experienced. Lauren could see it was hopeless to expect him to admit to any woman that he couldn't do without her, that he loved her, in so many words. And, yet, if he ever gave her the chance, Lauren knew she could show him the rich freedom of a love that trusted without grasping, without needing to possess utterly.

Watching the beloved face, Lauren decided there had been enough togetherness for one night. Mike was tired. Now that they had reached an agreement, an acceptance of each other's feelings, surely they could shift into a more relaxed mode of behavior? Was the testing period over? Perhaps the learning time could begin, the time when they might grow in under-

standing, in sensitivity, in the acknowledgment of who
they were.

All her experience with Al Rose, which admittedly
hadn't prepared her to deal with a man of Mike Landrill's
complexity and subtlety, advised her to return to her
own stateroom as soon as courtesy permitted, to let
Mike make the plans he wished for their future
association. She turned her attention to the food.

"I'd like to dress and go to my cabin now," she said
gently, when she had finished eating. "I'm really tired
and I need to be sure what's happening with the models.
You make me forget everything but you."

Mike looked dissatisfied, but he yielded graciously
enough to her request. He insisted upon dressing and
taking her to her door. It was well after midnight, but
the ship was still alive with light and the sound of
passengers celebrating the final hours of an exciting
voyage.

Mike saw her into her sitting room, gave her a mock-
ferocious glare, and muttered, "I'm not going to kiss
you goodnight. I know too well what *that* leads to."

He was darling and funny, and she adored him in
ways she had never suspected were possible while she
had been married to Al. I've learned about love, too,
she thought. You're really never finished learning.

She closed the door gently. Dani and Nella were not
in their bedroom, but Lauren didn't begrudge them
their night of triumph. Their loyalty had touched her
deeply; she had never experienced quite such a sense
of team-sharing.

I guess it takes a tragedy to bring out the strength in
people, the friendliness, she told herself. Thank good-
ness for Dani and Nella. And Derek and the troupe.

While she thought about it, Lauren wrote out the
check for their services, and added a bonus. With it she

wrote a note of thanks and, giving them her Los Angeles address, asked them to get in touch with her in case
they ever toured the States again. She signed her name,
then went to the phone on the off chance of finding
them in their cabin.

Two minutes later she was speaking to Violet. "We've
just got in, luv," the older woman told her. "Tony and
the chicks are still doing the rounds, but Derek and I
are getting past it."

There was a protest, clearly audible, from her spouse
in the background. Lauren laughed. "Where are you?
I've got your check here and I think it's better to get it
to you tonight. The morning will probably bring its
own confusions."

Violet gave her directions. Lauren collected three of
her signature silk scarves for the women and on her way
to Violet's cabin, a bottle of Chivas Regal for the men.

Half an hour later, she was walking down her corridor toward her suite. A man's form detached itself
from the wall. It was Mike. He looked very serious,
almost stern. Lauren's heart sank. Not second thoughts.
Oh, no.

Without greeting her by name, he said abruptly, "Do
you remember what I said to you about not kissing you
good night?"

Lauren nodded.

"I was wrong," Mike said, and proceeded to kiss her
with such passionate sweetness that her heart seemed
to be melting in her breast. Finally he lifted his head.

"That's better. I can go to sleep now."

Lauren couldn't help grinning. "I'm not sure *I* can,"
she said. "You're pretty potent, my friend."

"By the way, where have you been?" Mike asked,
trying to look unconcerned. "I've been standing here
for twenty minutes."

"I took the check to my dancers," Lauren told him. "Trying to thank them for saving my show. They were wonderful, weren't they?"

Mike nodded agreement, and then stood staring at her. Lauren said nothing. It still surprised her to realize how satisfying it was just standing beside this man. She didn't even need to speak. After a minute Mike shook his head, once, quickly.

"We're like two adolescents after the prom," he said, "I hate to say good night to you, Lauren."

"The night we met—ye gods, was it only four days ago—you quoted Juliet to me. 'Parting is such sweet sorrow/ That I shall say good night till it be morrow.' "

"Don't tempt me, lady," muttered the man.

Lauren went on. "And *then* you quoted Romeo—"

Mike took up the quotation. " 'Sleep dwell upon thine eyes/ peace in thy breast! Would I were sleep and peace, so sweet to rest!' "

Lauren's breath caught in her throat. This was the man who had called *her* a romantic. That greedy starlet had a lot to answer for. But he was changing—he *was*. At that moment Lauren would have done anything Mike asked her. She looked up at him with all her love in her face, clear to see.

Mike held her shoulders lightly with his hands, bent over her, and kissed her once, gently, on the lips. "Soon," he said, and turned and walked away.

It took Lauren a long time to get to sleep.

Chapter Nine

The morning sped by in a whirlwind of packing and last-minute decisions. Lauren instructed the purser's office to throw her wine-stained costumes overboard, or dispose of them in any other way that suited them. She carefully packed the survivors, and then unpacked them and offered them to the models and the three dancers. When Dani and Nella had each chosen a favorite—Nella wanted the cloak, for some reason—Lauren sent the rest to the Stranges' stateroom. She knew that Violet would seize upon the bronze silk with true delight.

Then there was their own packing to do. She had to help the models, as she had expected. Vails had to be set aside for the stewards and stewardesses who had been so tireless in securing their comfort.

Then came the moment when Lauren had to tell her models that she wasn't going to be staying at the Bristol with them. To her surprise and chagrin, she found that both of them had expected some such development. They reassured her that they would manage very nicely alone. Lauren, subdued by so much worldliness, handed them their return-flight tickets.

Dani confiscated them at once. "I'll look after these," she declared. Nella nodded happily.

Then Lauren told them of the car and driver that

Mike was putting at their disposal. "Just be ready when the driver comes for you on Sunday," she warned. "I wouldn't want you to be left behind." She glanced at them with concern. She was so used to managing things for them that she didn't quite picture them coping on their own. "Have you enough cash for your meals and extras?"

"Yes, Mother." Dani grinned. Lauren was reminded of Mike's comment. She apologized for acting like a mother hen, and the models forgave her.

They decided to eat breakfast in the dining room with the troupe, and the meal became a pleasant leave-taking. Lauren was hoping that she would never have to encounter Herbert again, but he was waiting for her outside the Tables of the World restaurant. He didn't seem guilty or embarrassed. She decided to be civilized.

"Well, Lauren, you were lucky," was his charming opening gambit. "Even winning a consolation prize."

There was little to say in answer to such a back-handed compliment. "Thank you," she said dryly.

"How are you going to handle the return trip?" he went on.

"It's all arranged," Lauren told him.

"Well, have a good time in London," Herbert taunted. "I wouldn't want to have to ride herd on those two cows."

Lauren turned away without another word. Herbert wasn't worth it.

Their steward had been specially requested, he told her, to see that their baggage was taken to the train. "Please don't worry, madam, it's all taken care of," he said confidently. Lauren relaxed and luxuriated in Mike's providence.

She made her good-byes to the models in their sitting room before they went on deck to disembark. "That way we won't be trying to keep in touch in the crowd," she explained. The models were really sorry to part with her; their evident affection moved Lauren. With many good wishes for their future success, and an urgent request to look her up soon after they returned to Los Angeles, she sent them ahead of her to disembark.

Half an hour later she walked toward the boat train. Someone came up behind her and took her arm.

"There you are," Mike said with satisfaction. "Everything all right?"

"Yes, thank you." Lauren was too happy to say any more.

They were almost safe on the train when the reporters found them. Lauren, who hadn't expected much notice—after all, as Herbert had reminded her, her award was in the nature of a consolation prize—was shocked at the strident and often impertinent questions Mike was fielding. It wasn't all velvet, being such a wealthy and notable man, she decided.

And then one of the reporters called out, "Is that your current playmate, Mr. Landrill? What's her name?"

Mike strode forward to stand directly in front of the fellow. "Would you like to apologize or would you prefer a sock in the jaw?" Mike asked quietly.

Only those reporters standing directly beside the offender heard him. They moved back out of the way, but just a little, keeping their front seats for the fight.

The man took a good look at Mike's narrowed eyes and large fists, and backed away. "Sorry, ma'am." He flicked a calculating glance at Lauren. "I just wanted to know the name of Mr. Landrill's latest, ah, popsy. *Now!*" He caught the fury in Mike's eyes, waved his hand, and a flashbulb exploded. "Thanks."

"This lady is my fiancée," Mike said grimly. "We shall

be married soon. Now get the hell out of my way before I walk over you."

Without further comment to the crowd of avid reporters who followed, yelling questions, Mike put his arm around Lauren's shoulders and led her to one of the first-class carriages. He slammed the door in the faces of the press hounds and helped Lauren to a seat, taking the one between her and the window. Then he smiled.

"I warned you we'd have to run the gauntlet," he said wryly. Then he watched her face. He seemed to be waiting for something.

Lauren hadn't been able to think clearly since Mike's announcement. Of course she knew it was a face-saver, but still it was such a massive defense—like hitting a flea with a pile driver. She nodded at him, and then looked around her to avoid meeting his eyes.

There were several other travelers in their section, none of whom, with true British decorum, was so much as glancing at the latest arrivals. Mike caught her eye and smiled.

"A delightful change from those importunate pests," he said in a passable imitation of an Oxford accent. He was rewarded by a grunt of agreement from behind an open newspaper.

He kept his eyes on Lauren's face, waiting for her to say something, but she was too confused to know how to deal with the problem. No, she admitted, she *wanted* his comment to be true and hated to say anything that might close off the possibility that he meant it.

The rest of the short trip was accomplished in silence. Mike made no more overtures; his face was shuttered and tired-looking. Lauren was too stunned to speak. When they reached the station, Mike was recognized as they made their way to the street by a uniformed chauffeur, who got them and their bags settled in a limousine with the minimum of trouble. A glass partition gave them privacy. Lauren leaned back with a sigh compounded of relief at being alone with Mike and apprehension at his continued silence. Why didn't he open the conversation? Why didn't he say something?

On the way to the hotel, Mike continued to brood. Lauren made up her mind that he was unhappy at his impulsive declaration to the press. Should she reassure him that she wouldn't hold him to it? She wished so desperately that it was true that she found it difficult to bring up the subject. She stared out her window, frowning and thinking so hard that she didn't see the bright streets through which they were passing.

Gradually she became aware of a feeling of stress in the closed compartment. Perhaps it was the quality of the silence, which seemed to change and become electric; perhaps it was a difference in the position and stance of the man's big body seated so close to hers in the car. At any rate, Lauren realized that Mike was under an increasing tension of some sort. She turned her head to glance at him, and was shocked to perceive that he was in a flaming temper.

She opened her mouth to ask what was wrong, and couldn't. His narrow-eyed glare robbed her of speech. Yet when his first remark came, it was delivered not with anger but with ice-cold sarcasm.

"You've done it to me, haven't you? Succeeded where all the other greedy ladies failed? Now I suppose you've got the wedding, the honeymoon, and the divorce settlements all planned?"

From trembling hope and fear Lauren was driven into unbridled anger. "I said nothing. *You* were the one who told the reporters—"

"You knew I wouldn't let them foul-mouth you," he snapped.

"I had no idea they would say anything about me at all. I'm pretty small potatoes compared to the great Mr. Landrill. If you feel that angry at the idea of marriage, you shouldn't have said what you did."

"I didn't hear you denying it. Either to them or to me while we were on the train. I waited for you to repeat what you'd said last night about not bargaining or demanding a ring, but not a word. Then I thought you didn't want to discuss our private business in front of the Britishers, so I waited for us to be alone here in the car. But no, clever Mrs. Rose has got what she's been angling for ever since she found out who I was. Or had you looked me up before you left Los Angeles?"

This was a nightmare. Lauren could hardly recognize the man beside her as the one who had made love so passionately on the ship. There was only one thing to do.

"Of course, I'm not going to marry you. I don't—"

He cut her short. Apparently he was so angry that he hadn't even heard her rejection.

"My father and mother destroyed each other—he, by his callous neglect of her, she by her greed and cold nature. Lilith took me to the cleaners emotionally even worse than she did financially. She had a dozen lovers, male and female. She'd pick up with my best friends. For two years after I got rid of her, I couldn't look at a woman without wanting to vomit. And now Buffy is doing the same number on my brother. Women! You're disgusting."

Lauren could have protested that she was not his mother or Lilith or Buffy, but what was the use? Her failure to reject the announcement he'd made to the reporters had damned her in Mike's eyes. He was so afraid of being trapped and then destroyed that he wasn't ready to hear anything she could say. So she kept very quiet and stared straight ahead. Even when Mike snarled, "Well?" at her, she resisted the urge to explain, to comfort. He would only think it was another move in a campaign to get power over him.

"I was right, then," he snapped as the limousine drew up in front of the Ritz. "It's a good thing I found out so quickly."

He got out and stalked into the hotel without waiting for Lauren. There were three reporters hanging around the entrance, and they followed at his heels, yelping questions.

The chauffeur had opened the trunk and was taking out the bags. Lauren went to him, took her case, smiled her thanks—she couldn't manage to speak—and looked around for a taxi. She saw one and gestured the driver over.

The chauffeur appeared at her shoulder, a worried expression on his face.

Lauren found her voice. "It's all right. I've thanked Mr. Landrill for the lift. Thank you, also."

She climbed up into the big boxlike cab. The chauffeur handed in her bag and shut the door. He still looked worried. He touched his cap to her as the cab drew away from the curb.

"Where to, miss?" asked the cabby.

"The Bristol Hotel, please," Lauren said. She was glad of the gloomy interior of the musty old cab. She could cry without anyone seeing her. But somehow, she didn't.

It was a very short trip to the Bristol. When she got there, she found that Dani and Nella hadn't checked in yet. Also no one had canceled her reservation, thank God. She signed the register and followed the bellboy up to her room. It was small, tastefully decorated, and empty. It also had a lock and key, which she used as soon as the boy had left her suitcases. Slowly she took off her clothing, dug into her suitcase for a nightgown, and got into bed.

I wish, she thought drearily, I was dead.

And then she cried. For a long time.

It was the telephone ringing that awakened her. She made no effort to answer it. However, a few minutes later, there was a pounding on the door. Lauren said nothing. And then Dani's voice, shrill enough to be heard through the door, called to her, "Lauren! Are you in there?"

Wearily, feeling more like a hundred than thirty-five, Lauren padded over and unlocked the door. Dani took one look at her face and grabbed her. "It's all right, Lauren, we're here now. Nella and I will look after you, poor baby."

Looking into those concerned brown eyes, Lauren felt the first break in the iron agony of grief that had held her imprisoned.

The models insisted that she accompany them to the theater. They had managed to get three tickets, they informed her proudly, to a hilariously funny show that had been running for nine years. Lauren glanced at her watch. Five o'clock. She forced a smile. Right now she wanted nothing more than to hide in her room until it was time to catch the plane for Los Angeles, but Dani and Nella's loyalty demanded a cheerful response.

"We'll have time to try some of that famous British high tea, then," she said.

"Time? No way," Dani advised her positively. "The show begins at six-thirty. I guess that's for the convenience of people who want to dine in style after the show, at nine or ten o'clock. But we're ravenous. We'll dress and have dinner before we go."

Hastily Lauren calculated. Shower, dress, eat, taxi to show. Between five and six-thirty?

"You're planning to snatch a bite in the coffee shop?" she asked.

Dani gave her a superior smile. "The Bristol Hotel doesn't have a coffee shop," she announced. "I already checked. But they do have a gorgeous maître d' and he says he'll serve us dinner if we get there by five-thirty. Not all their guests want to wait till ten o'clock to have a meal."

Lauren couldn't help smiling. Dani was incorrigible. Lauren only hoped it wouldn't occur to her to ask some handsome guard at Buckingham Palace to give her a private tour.

All through the elegant meal served in the Bristol's spacious dining room, Dani and Nella chatted excitedly. There were only two other tables occupied. At one sat an elderly couple in tweeds, who apparently had nothing to say to one another, but ate every course with relish. At the other table sat two men in faultless evening dress. One of them was a good-looking middle-aged man. To Dani's dissatisfaction, neither of them spared a look at the other diners, but instead carried on a low-voiced, intense argument throughout the meal.

The food was superb: lobster bisque, Cornish game hens, asparagus, accompanied by a fine white wine, and then raspberries in thick cream. They had no time to linger over coffee. Lauren signed for the meal and left a generous tip. Dani had been right. She was welcoming the trip to the theater, since no one could reach her by phone or in person while she was there.

And then she thought bitterly, who am I trying to fool? I'm just afraid he won't want to reach me ever again. And I don't want to sit around waiting for him *not* to call.

Dani noted the bitter droop to Lauren's lips but said nothing. She didn't believe in asking questions about personal troubles. She told herself she might have to do something if she knew the score, but that cynical attitude was just a pose. She really couldn't bear to see anyone hurt. Not knowing was a defense. She urged Lauren to get a taxi so they could get to the theater before curtain time.

"It's only six o'clock," protested Lauren. "The way we raced through that meal, the maître d' will never forgive us."

Lauren found herself laughing with her friends at the naughty, funny play. Nella bought chocolates and tea in the intermission. They were still chuckling over certain lines and actions in the play as they got out of the taxi and went into the small but luxurious lobby at the hotel. "Thank you for tonight. I really enjoyed it," Lauren said.

They got their keys and went toward the elevator.

"They call it a *lift* here," Nella whispered.

"Well, it does," argued Dani, who already showed signs of becoming an Anglo-phile. "I'd rather be lifted than elevated."

While Nella was puzzling this out, they reached their floor and went toward their rooms. Taped on Lauren's door was a large, official-looking envelope. Lauren took it down, opened her door, and said good night to the models. Nella looked anxious, but Dani pushed her into their room, which was next to Lauren's.

With her door locked behind her, Lauren opened the envelope with shaking fingers. Whatever he had to say, she wasn't going to get mixed up with Mike Landrill ever again. It hurt too much. She took a deep breath.

She had to know what the note said, even at the risk of further pain. She took the folded letter out of the envelope. A slip of paper fell out to the floor. Absently, Lauren bent to retrieve it. And then she saw what it was.

It was a check for twenty thousand dollars. And it was made out to Lauren Rose, and signed, in a slashing hand, Mike Landrill.

Lauren felt such a gust of rage that she shook with it. That bastard. That rotten excuse for a human being. How dare he send her money to pay her off as though she were some cheap tramp! Not pausing to reflect that at twenty thousand, the tramp could hardly be called cheap, Lauren jammed the unread letter and the check into her handbag and almost ran back downstairs and out of the hotel.

There was a taxi waiting near the entrance. Lauren flagged it imperiously.

"The Ritz," she snapped.

Her seething rage hadn't had time to cool down when she was deposited in front of his hotel. She strode into the lobby, and demanded to be told the number of Mr. Landrill's suite.

"Is he expecting you, madame?" enquired the clerk.

"Oh, yes," said Lauren loftily. She would have told any lie in the book in order to throw the check in his rotten face.

When she had the number, Lauren lost no time in going up to the correct floor. She strode along the corridor, her anger carrying her. When she reached the door, she hammered on it with her fist and then turned the handle. It gave. She flung the door open.

"What kept you?"

Michael Landrill was lounging on a comfortable-looking couch, dressed in the dark-blue robe she well remembered. Near him was a trolley loaded with silver chafing dishes and trays of food. Coffee bubbled in a percolator, its fragrance mouth-watering.

Mike stood up with a grin. "I knew the check would bring you if the note didn't."

Lauren was dizzy with the conflict of emotions that pounded at her brain. "What note? I didn't read the letter. When I saw that check I could have—I could have—"

"Thanked me nicely?" There was derisive laughter in his words, but his eyes held a light Lauren didn't understand. "Kissed me? Killed me?"

Lauren gritted her teeth. "Of all the rotten, low-down, creeps I ever met." She drew a breath. "If you think you're going to give me money for what was between us, you've got another think coming. All I want to do is forget that I ever met you."

"That's going to be kind of hard," Mike said in a surprisingly calm voice.

It caught Lauren's attention. "What do you mean?" she asked suspiciously.

"Well, if we're going on a honeymoon, we sure can't pretend we don't know each other. People would think it was peculiar," he added in a tone of kindly explanation.

Lauren gaped at him. Was he crazy? What was this about honeymoons?

The man actually laughed! Lauren surged forward, her hand raised to strike the laughter off his mocking face. He caught it, and since it held her purse, he took that from her and opened it. He extracted the letter.

"I knew you'd bring it," he said, pleased. "You probably intended stuffing it down my throat."

"How right you are," Lauren snapped.

"Did you read the letter?" Mike persisted.

"No! The check fell out and I saw it. I got so angry—"

Mike grinned. "It worked, didn't it? I knew that if
the note didn't—"

Lauren snatched the note out of his hands rudely.
She flipped it open. It read:

Dear Lauren,

Please come to the Ritz and let me beg your
pardon properly for the foolish, stupid, childish
act I put on this afternoon. I guess it was the last
strikeback of a bitter conditioned reflex I've been
saddled with since I was a kid.

Or perhaps it was bridal nerves?

Anyway, I've been fighting it out in my mind,
and the answer is simple. I've got to marry you, so
I can have exclusive rights to giving you your
showers. Also feeding you midnight suppers, and
swimming with you at the crack of dawn, and maybe
letting you win a few more races. Also I can't
jeopardize my chances of signing you for Landrill's,
exclusively. My lawyer would never forgive me if I
lost him our chance at September Song! To say
nothing of my chef, who feels he has never been
properly appreciated.

So please come, Lauren.

I beg you. My lawyer begs you. My chef begs
you—or would, if he realized the problem.

If you say no to this triple plea, then take the money and spend it on a smear campaign of Landrill's;
or buy Herbert an exploding cigar. Or something.

I hope you'll come. Because I love you.

Lauren folded the note slowly. She wanted to look at
him, and yet she was almost afraid to. What would she
see on his face?

And then, suddenly, it didn't matter. Because she loved him so desperately that nothing in life would ever have been truly joyous again if she had lost him.

She dropped the letter and faced him fully. And he wasn't laughing. There was a look she had never seen before, a searching, hopeful, vulnerable sweetness and appeal that broke down every defense she might have erected. She ran to him, and his arms were open and ready when she reached him.

"Oh, Lauren," he said, and his deep voice trembled with the love and relief he felt. "Oh, Lauren, thank God. I thought I'd blown the one chance I've ever had at the real thing."

His kiss, hard and demanding, expressed his need. And then it softened, and became deliciously seductive. Lauren opened her love-drugged eyes. He was smiling down at her, so pleased and satisfied at the success of his stratagem that she had to chuckle.

"You said, once," he stated, "that you didn't want a shipboard romance. Well, I'm afraid you're going to have to settle for one." He waited, eyes glinting with mischief, for the expected flare-up.

Lauren smiled demurely. She *trusted* the guy. Still, not to spoil his joke, she said, "What do you mean, shipboard romance?"

He laughed triumphantly. "I've just booked us for the *Queen Elizabeth*'s world tour. And am I going to romance you for three months!"

"I love you, too," Lauren whispered.

TELL US YOUR OPINIONS AND RECEIVE A FREE COPY
OF THE RAPTURE NEWSLETTER.

Thank you for filling out our questionnaire. Your response to the following questions will help us to bring you more and better books. In appreciation of your help we will send you a free copy of the Rapture Newsletter.

1. Book Title:_____

   Book #:_____ (5–7)

2. Using the scale below how would you rate this book on the following features? Please write in one rating from 0–10 for each feature in the spaces provided. Ignore bracketed numbers.

(Poor) 0 1 2 3 4 5 6 7 8 9 10 (Excellent)
                                   0–10 Rating

Overall Opinion of Book. . . . . _____ (8)
Plot/Story. . . . . _____ (9)
Setting/Location. . . . . _____ (10)
Writing Style. . . . . _____ (11)
Dialogue. . . . . _____ (12)
Love Scenes. . . . . _____ (13)
Character Development:
Heroine:. . . . . _____ (14)
Hero:. . . . . _____ (15)
Romantic Scene on Front Cover. . . . . _____ (16)
Back Cover Story Outline . . . . _____ (17)
First Page Excerpts. . . . . _____ (18)

3. What is your: Education: Age: _____ (20-22)

       High School (   )1   4 Yrs. College (   )3
       2 Yrs. College (   )2 Post Grad   (   )4 (23)

4. Print Name:_____

   Address:_____

   City:_____State:_____Zip:_____

   Phone # (   )_____(25)

   Thank you for your time and effort. Please send to New American Library, Rapture Romance Research Department, 1633 Broadway, New York, NY 10019.

RAPTURE ROMANCE

**Provocative and sensual,
passionate and tender—
the magic and mystery of love
in all its many guises**

Coming next month

PASSION'S PROMISE by Sharon Wagner. When her long-ago first love Ben Cumberland reentered her life, Joyce Cole felt all her defenses crumbling. But would the passion he promised cost her the independence she'd worked so long to achieve. . . ?

SILK AND STEEL by Kathryn Kent. Though their wills clashed by day, at night Ryan and Laura were joined in sweet ecstasy. But did the successful promoter really love the young fashion designer—or was he only using her talents to settle an old business score?

ELUSIVE PARADISE by Eleanor Frost. For Anne and Jeremy, a private business relationship turned into an emotional, passionate affair—that was soon the focus of a magazine article. Then Anne began to wonder if Jeremy was interested in her, or publicity for their business venture . . .

RED SKY AT NIGHT by Ellie Winslow. Could Nat Langley fulfill trucker Kay O'Hara's every dream? Nat had designed the rig she'd always wanted, and Kay had to find out whether he was trying to sell himself—or his truck—to her . . .

BITTERSWEET TEMPTATION by Jillian Roth. Chase Kincaid haunted Julie King's thoughts long after he'd broken her heart. Now he was back, reawakening dreams and desires, making her fear she'd be hurt again . . .

RECKLESS DESIRE by Nelle Russell. Novelist Justin Reynolds was the most magnetic male Margot Abbott had ever met. But what kind of love story were his caresses creating for Margot, who knew him so little yet wanted him so much. . . ?

GET SIX RAPTURE ROMANCES EVERY MONTH FOR THE PRICE OF FIVE.

Subscribe to Rapture Romance and every month you'll get six new books for the price of five. That's an $11.70 value for just $9.75. We're so sure you'll love them, we'll give you 10 days to look them over at home. Then you can keep all six and pay for only five, or return the books and owe nothing.

To start you off, we'll send you four books absolutely FREE. "Apache Tears," "Love's Gilded Mask," "O'Hara's Woman," and "Love So Fearful." The total value of all four books is $7.80, but they're yours *free* even if you never buy another book.

So order Rapture Romances today. And prepare to meet a different breed of man.

YOUR FIRST 4 BOOKS ARE FREE!
JUST PHONE 1-800-228-1888*

(Or mail the coupon below)
*In Nebraska call 1-800-642-8788

- -

Rapture Romance, P.O. Box 996, Greens Farms, CT 06436

Please send me the 4 Rapture Romances described in this ad FREE and without obligation. Unless you hear from me after I receive them, send me 6 NEW Rapture Romances to preview each month. I understand that you will bill me for only 5 of them at $1.95 each (a total of $9.75) with no shipping, handling or other charges. I always get one book FREE every month. There is no minimum number of books I must buy, and I can cancel at any time. The first 4 FREE books are mine to keep even if I never buy another book.

Name	(please print)
Address	City
State Zip	Signature (if under 18, parent or guardian must sign)

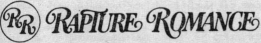

RAPTURE ROMANCE

This offer, limited to one per household and not valid to present subscribers, expires June 30, 1984. Prices subject to change. Specific titles subject to availability. Allow a minimum of 4 weeks for delivery.

RR 183

RAPTURE ROMANCE

Provocative and sensual, passionate and tender— the magic and mystery of love in all its many guises New Titles Available Now

(0451)

#45 ☐ **SEPTEMBER SONG by Lisa Moore.** Swearing her career came first, Lauren Rose faced the challenge of her life in Mark Landrill's arms, for she had to choose between the work she thrived on—and a passion that left her both fulfilled and enslaved . . . (126303—$1.95)*

#46 ☐ **A MOUNTAIN MAN by Megan Ashe.** For Kelly March, Josh Munroe's beloved mountain world was a haven where she could prove her independence. but Josh—who tormented her with desire—resented the intrusion. Could Kelly prove she was worth his love—and, if she did, would she lose all she'd fought to achieve? (126319—$1.95)*

#47 ☐ **THE KNAVE OF HEARTS by Estelle Edwards.** Brilliant young lawyer Kate Sewell had no defense against carefree riverboat gambler Hal Lewis. But could Kate risk her career— even for the ecstasy his love promised? (126327—$1.95)*

#48 ☐ **BEYOND ALL STARS by Melinda McKenzie.** For astronaut Ann Lafton, working with Commander Ed Saber brought emotional chaos that jeopardized their NASA shuttle mission. But Ann couldn't stop dreaming that this sensuous lover would fly her to the stars . . . (126335—$1.95)*

#49 ☐ **DREAMLOVER by JoAnn Robb.** Painter K.L. Michaels needed Hunter St. James to pull off a daring masquerade, but she didn't count on losing her relaxed lifestyle as their wild love affair unfolded. Could their nights of sensual fireworks make up for their daily battles? (126343—$1.95)*

#50 ☐ **A LOVE SO FRESH by Marilyn Davids.** Loving Ben Heron was everything Anna Markham needed. But she considered marriage a trap, and Ben, too, had been burned before. Passion drew them together, but was their rapture enough to overcome the obstacles they faced? (126351—$1.95)*

*Price is $2.25 in Canada

To order, use the convenient coupon on the next page.

RAPTURE ROMANCE

Provocative and sensual,
passionate and tender—
the magic and mystery of love
in all its many guises

Buy them at your local

bookstore or use coupon

on next page for ordering.

RAPTURE ROMANCE

Provocative and sensual, passionate and tender— the magic and mystery of love in all its many guises

SPECIAL $1.00 REBATE OFFER
WHEN YOU BUY
FOUR RAPTURE ROMANCES

To receive your cash refund, send:

1. This coupon: To qualify for the $1.00 refund, this coupon, completed with your name and address, must be used. (Certificate may not be reproduced)

2. Proof of purchase: Print, on the reverse side of this coupon, the *title* of the books, the *numbers* of the books (on the upper right hand of the front cover preceding the price), and the U.P.C. numbers (on the back covers) on your next four purchases.

3. Cash register receipts, with prices circled to:
   Rapture Romance $1.00 Refund Offer
   P.O. Box NB037
   El Paso, Texas 79977

Offer good only in the U.S. and Canada. Limit one refund/response per household for any group of four Rapture Romance titles. Void where prohibited, taxed or restricted. Allow 6–8 weeks for delivery. Offer expires March 31, 1984.

NAME_____

ADDRESS_____

CITY_____STATE_____ZIP_____

SPECIAL $1.00 REBATE OFFER
WHEN YOU BUY
FOUR RAPTURE ROMANCES

See complete details on reverse

1. Book Title _____

Book Number 451-_____

U.P.C. Number 7116200195-_____

2. Book Title _____

Book Number 451-_____

U.P.C. Number 7116200195-_____

3. Book Title _____

Book Number 451-_____

U.P.C. Number 7116200195-_____

4. Book Title _____

Book Number 451-_____

U.P.C. Number 7116200195-_____

U.P.C. Number

0   SAMPLE

71162 00195